'You can't shake off this novel; it gets lungs, breaks your heart. As allegory, as a ____ as vision and as art it is stunning.'

Christos Tsiolkas

'*The Natural Way of Things* is a brave, brilliant book. I would defy anyone to read it and not come out a changed person.'

Malcolm Knox, author of *The Wonder Lover* and *The Life*

'A fully imagined dystopian parable, vivid, insightful, the voices of young women echoing through the gum trees ...'

Joan London, author of *The Golden Age*

'This is a stunning exploration of ambiguities – of power, of morality, of judgement ... It will not leave you easily; it took my breath away.'

Ashley Hay, author of *The Railwayman's Wife*

'Few other novels have captured the stain of misogyny quite like Charlotte Wood's *The Natural Way of Things* ... Terrifying, remarkable and utterly unforgettable.'

Clementine Ford

'*The Natural Way of Things* is both harrowing and gorgeous. It feels, at times, like a nightmare; but one in which women make serious pacts, take serious pleasures, and reimagine what it might mean to live in the world. I feel as if I've been witness to the most terrible injustice, but also the most astonishing beauty.'

Fiona McFarlane, author of *The Night Guest* and *The High Places*

THE NATURAL WAY OF THINGS

CHARLOTTE WOOD

ALLEN&UNWIN

First published in Great Britain in 2016 by Allen & Unwin
First published in Australia in 2015 by Allen & Unwin
This paperback edition published in 2017

Allen & Unwin
c/o Atlantic Books
Ormond House
26–27 Boswell Street
London WC1N 3JZ

Phone: 020 7269 1610
Fax: 020 7430 0916
Email: UK@allenandunwin.com
Web: www.allenandunwin.com/uk

A CIP catalogue record of this book is available from the British Library.

Paperback ISBN 978 1 76029 191 4
E-book ISBN 978 1 92526 861 4

Internal design by Lisa White
Set in 12.5/19 pt Fairfield LH by Bookhouse, Sydney
Printed in Great Britain by Clays Ltd, St Ives plc

10 9 8 7 6 5 4 3 2 1

part one:
SUMMER

SO THERE were kookaburras here. This was the first thing Yolanda knew in the dark morning. (That and *where's my durries?*) Two birds breaking out in that loose, sharp cackle, a bird call before the sun was up, loud and lunatic.

She got out of the bed and felt gritty boards beneath her feet. There was the coarse unfamiliar fabric of a nightdress on her skin. Who had put this on her?

She stepped across the dry wooden floorboards and stood, craning her neck to see through the high narrow space of a small window. The two streetlights she had seen in her dream turned out to be two enormous stars in a deep blue sky. The kookaburras dazzled the darkness with their horrible noise.

Later there would be other birds; sometimes she would ask about them, but questions made people suspicious and they wouldn't answer her. She would begin to make up her

3

own names for the birds. The waterfall birds, whose calls fell tumbling. And the squeakers, the tiny darting grey ones. Who would have known there could be so many birds in the middle of absolutely fucking nowhere?

But that would all come later.

Here, on this first morning, before everything began, she stared up at the sky as the blue night lightened, and listened to the kookaburras and thought, *Oh, yes, you are right.* She had been delivered to an asylum.

She groped her way along the walls to a door. But there was no handle. She felt at its edge with her fingernails: locked. She climbed back into the bed and pulled the sheet and blanket up to her neck. Perhaps they were right. Perhaps she was mad, and all would be well.

She knew she was not mad, but all lunatics thought that.

When they were small she and Darren had once collected mounds of moss from under the tap at the back of the flats, in the dank corner of the yard where it was always cool, even on the hottest days. They prised up the clumps of moss, the earth heavy in their fingers, and it was a satisfying job, lifting a corner and being careful not to crack the lump, getting better as they went at not splitting the moss and pulling it to pieces. They filled a crackled orange plastic bucket with the moss and took it out to the verge on the street to sell. 'Moss for sale!' they screamed at the hot cars going by, giggling and gesturing and clowning, and, 'Wouldja like ta buy some moss?' more politely if a man or woman walked past. Nobody bought any moss, even when they spread it beautifully along the verge, and Darren sent Yolanda back twice for water to pour over it, to keep it springy to the touch. Then they got too hot, and Darren left her there sitting on the verge while he went and fetched two cups of water, but still nobody bought any moss. So they climbed the stairs and went inside to watch TV, and the moss dried out and turned grey and dusty and died.

This was what the nightdress made her think of, the dead moss, and she loved Darren even though she knew it was him who let them bring her here, wherever she was. Perhaps he had put her in the crazed orange bucket and brought her here himself.

What she really needed was a ciggy.

While she waited there in the bed, in the dead-moss nightdress and the wide silence—the kookaburras stopped as instantly as they began—she took an inventory of herself.

Yolanda Kovacs, nineteen years eight months. Good body (she was just being honest, why would she boast, when it had got her into such trouble?). She pulled the rustling nightdress closer—it scratched less, she was discovering, when tightly wrapped.

One mother, one brother, living. One father, unknown, dead or alive. One boyfriend, Robbie, who no longer believed her (at poor Robbie, the rush of a sob in her throat. She swallowed it down). One night, one dark room, that bastard and his mates, one terrible mistake. And then one giant fucking unholy mess.

Yolanda Kovacs, lunatic. And that word frightened her, and she turned her face and cried into the hard pillow.

She stopped crying and went on with her inventory. Things missing: handbag, obviously. Ciggies (almost full pack), purple lighter, phone, make-up, blue top, bra, underpants, skinny jeans. Shoes. Three silver rings from Bali, reindeer necklace from Darren (she patted her chest for it again, still gone).

Yolanda looked up at the dark window. *Oh, stars. Stay with me.* But very soon the sky was light and the two stars had gone, completely.

She breathed in and out, longed for nicotine, curled in the bed, watching the door.

IN A patch of sunlight Verla sits on a wooden folding chair and waits. When the door opens she holds her breath. It is another girl who comes into the room. They lock eyes for an instant, then look away to the floor, the walls.

The girl moves stiffly in her weird costume, taking only a few steps into the room. The door has closed behind her. The only spare chair is beside Verla's, so Verla gets up and moves to the window. It is too much, that she be put so close to a stranger. She stands at the window, looking out through a fly-spotted pane at nothing. There is bright sunlight coming into the room, but only reflected off the white weatherboards of another building just metres away. She presses her face to the glass but can see no windows anywhere along the length of that building.

She can feel the other girl behind her in the room, staring at her peculiar clothes. The stiff long green canvas smock, the

7

coarse calico blouse beneath, the hard brown leather boots and long woollen socks. The ancient underwear. It is summer. Verla sweats inside them. She can feel it dawning on the other girl that she is a mirror: that she too wears this absurd costume, looks as strange as Verla does.

Verla tries to work out what it was she had been given, scanning back through the vocabulary of her father's sedatives. Midazolam, Largactil? She wants to live. She tries wading through memory, logic, but can't grasp anything but the fact that all her own clothes—and, she supposes, the other girl's—are gone. She blinks a slow glance at the girl. Tall, heavy-lidded eyes, thick brows, long black hair to her waist is all Verla sees before looking away again. But she knows the girl stands there dumbly with her hands by her sides, staring down at the floorboards. Drugged too, Verla can tell from her slowness, her vacancy—this runaway, schoolgirl, drug addict? Nun, for all Verla knows. But somehow, even in this sweeping glance, the girl seems familiar.

She understands fear should be thrumming through her now. But logic is impossible, all thinking still glazed with whatever they have given her. Like the burred head on a screw, her thoughts can find no purchase.

Verla follows the girl's gaze. The floorboards glisten like honey in the sun. She has an impulse to lick them. She understands that fear is the only thing now that could conceivably save her from what is to come. But she is cotton-headed, too slow for that. The drug has dissolved adrenaline so completely it almost seems unsurprising to be here, with a stranger, in a strange room, wearing this bizarre olden-day costume. She can do nothing to resist it, cannot understand nor question. It is a kind of dumb relief.

But she can listen. Verla strains through her sedation. Somewhere beyond the door is the judder of some domestic motor—a fridge, maybe, or an air-conditioning unit. But the place is stinking hot, primitive. She has no idea where they are.

The room is large and light. There are the two wooden folding chairs—empty, the other girl did not sit—against a wall painted milky green, and a blackboard at the other end of the room with a rolled vinyl blind high up at the top of the board. Verla knows without knowing that if she tugged on the ring dangling from the centre of the blind she would pull down a map of Australia, coloured yellow and orange with blue water all around. The map would be faintly shiny and faintly creased from all the years of rolling up and down, and would somewhere contain the truth of where she has travelled to all those hours. When her mind is in order again she will be able to think. She will work it out, she will take charge of herself, will demand information and go to the highest authority and not rest and somehow get to the bottom of this fact of appearing to have been abducted right into the middle of the nineteen fucking fifties.

Outside, a single white cockatoo shrieks, closer and louder until the sound of it fills the room like murder. She and the girl lock gazes again, and then Verla peers back outside, up at the slot of sky. The bird flaps across the space between the buildings and then is gone.

She tries again, and this time through her sticky, jellied recollection Verla drags up the looming shape of a vehicle in the night. Is this recall, or dream? A bus. Gleaming yellow in the gloom. Purposeful, firm hands lifting and pushing at her. Waking at some time in the dark, unfamiliar velour of upholstery against her cheek. Headlights illuminating a long, straight, empty road. Did she stand up, swaying? Did she shout, was she pressed down? She rubs her wrist at the dream-memory of handcuff and rail.

Impossible.

Another dream sense—being hauled from the bus, held up, trying to speak, rough hands gripping, tasting dust in the dry and staticky night. She was far from home.

Now here she is, in this room.

Verla listens hard again. It now seems listening might be her only hope. She hears the creak somewhere of a door, a bird's cheeping. There will be a car engine, a plane, a train, something to locate them. There will be footsteps, talking, the presence of people in other rooms. She stares out the window at the weatherboards. There is nothing. The motor jerks—it is a fridge—and clicks off.

Now there is no sound at all but the other girl's slow, solid breathing. She has moved to sit, on one of the chairs. She sits with her legs apart, her forehead in her hands, elbows on her knees. Her black hair a curtain, reaching almost to the floor.

Verla wants to lie down on the floorboards and sleep. But some ancient instinct claws its way to the surface of consciousness, and she forces herself to stay upright. Minutes pass, or hours.

At last the other girl speaks, her voice thick and throaty. 'Have you got a cigarette?'

When Verla turns to her she sees how fresh the girl is, how young. And, again, familiar. It seems to Verla she has known this girl once, long ago. As if Verla had once owned then abandoned her, like a doll or a dog. And here she is, returned, an actor on a stage, and Verla there too, both of them

11

dressed in these strange prairie puppets' clothes. It could all be hallucination. But Verla knows it isn't. The doll opens her mouth to speak again and Verla says, 'No,' at the same time as the doll-or-dog girl asks, 'Do you know where we are?'

There are voices beyond the door in the hallway and in a sudden rush of clarity Verla realises she should have asked the girl where she has come from just now, what is outside the door, realises she has squandered her last chance to know what is to come. But it is too late. The voices are men's, loud, cheerful, workaday. Just before the door opens the other girl darts across the room to Verla's side, so they stand together facing the door, their backs to the window. As the door opens the two girls' hands find and close over each other.

A man clomps into the room. Sounds of life and movement bloom up the hallway behind him: another man's voice, the sound of moving cutlery, or knives. Delicate metal sounds, instruments clattering into a sink or bowl.

Verla's legs weaken; she might drop. The other girl's grip tightens over hers and Verla is surprised to learn this: *She is stronger than me.*

'Hey,' the man calls mildly, as if he is embarrassed to come across them there. Thick brown dreadlocks fall to his shoulders, framing a hippie boy's vacant, golden face. He shifts in his blue boiler suit, big black boots on his feet. The suit and the boots look new. He is uncomfortable in them. He stands with his arms folded, leaning back now and then to look out the door, waiting for someone.

He looks at them again, appraising them in their stiff, weird clothes. Curious objects. 'You must feel like shit, I s'pose.' A husky, lazy, pot-smoker's voice. He stretches, raising his arms high above him with his palms together, then dropping from the waist, head touching his knees, palms on the floor, he breathes, long and smoothly. *Salute to the sun*, Verla thinks. Then the man straightens up and sighs again, bored.

'It'll wear off soon, apparently,' he murmurs as if to himself, glancing out the door again.

The girls stay where they are, hands gripping.

Now another boiler suit strides into the room. Bustling, purposeful.

'Right,' he says. 'Who wants to go first?'

PROPPED UP against the windowsill, holding that other girl's hand to stop her falling to the ground, Yolanda felt her throat raw and thick as though something had been forced down her gullet while she slept. It hurt her a little to speak, but she heard herself say, 'I'll go first.'

For what, she didn't know. Only prayed they would crank up the dose of this shit first, and if not she would spit and claw until they did. The man came to her and bent to clip a little lead to a metal ring at the waist of her tunic (she hadn't noticed it until then), which made her let go that chick's hand. For the first time she looked at the other girl properly, standing there against the window with the light haloing her soft reddish-brown curls. Her blue eyes widening in terror, her freckled cheeks paling even whiter than the light outside. Yolanda wanted to say, *I'm the one being taken, you dumb bitch, it isn't happening to you.*

But she knew she was taking the easier path: she would find out what was coming while that girl endured another minute or hour or year in that room, waiting.

When the man sat her in the next room and clipped the other end of her leash to that heavy pedestal chair and then left, she looked around for wires and plugs, for fuck knew what else. She was facing death, maybe torture first. She began screaming for drugs.

When she came to again—she was getting used to the fade, out and in—she became conscious of several things. That it was the stoner with the dreads standing in front, then behind her, and that in his hand flashed a glint of steel. She closed her eyes in the thundering slosh of nausea—and then adrenaline exploded into relief, her innards turning to water, as she understood her throat was not to be slit.

She was getting a haircut.

In the relief she slumped and yes, nearly shat herself but didn't, just went out to it again until it was over. For those moments she felt only the oily, woolly tips of the stoner's dreads brushing against her neck and shoulders as he worked. Felt her head tugged at and released, tugged and released, surrendering to the touch as the scissors ground away at her hair, and she felt each new hank of cooler air arrive on her skin where hair used to be.

In the flooding relief—it was a liquid, heavy and cold and silver like lead, like another kind of drug—she thought, *that poor girl* back there. But also despised her for the way her fear had leaked and spread. *Find someone else's fucking hand to hold*, was what Yolanda thought then, there in the chair, closing her eyes again.

She heard the stoner murmur, 'These scissors are fucken blunt.' And Yolanda swore there were footsteps, skittery female footsteps, behind her on the lino floor. She could smell a woman, a cosmetic female smell, and heard a soft giggle, and then that all sank away and Yolanda with it, until the cold burr of an electric razor began at the nape of her neck, shocking her awake once more.

If there had been any woman she was gone. There was only the stoner again, breathing down over his work, *shaving* her head now, tracing her skull, making wide tracks with the razor on her fine, fine skin. Yolanda gasped aloud at the feel of her own half-shorn head. The razor stopped for a moment, held in mid-air. The stoner looked at her, irritable. He frowned and said, 'Shut up.' And then experimentally, as if testing the word, as if he'd never said it before, had just learned it, added, 'You slut.'

She looked down at the floor. Hair was only hair, as it fell. But there was so much of it, first in long shining straps, then little glossy black humps so the floorboards were covered in small dark creatures, waiting to be brought to life there on the ground.

When it was done the man stepped back, flexed his shoulders and stretched his arms high above him again, like he'd done in the other room. The razor glinted in his hand—he was bored again, and tiring. He unclipped the leash and shoved at the chair so it jolted forwards, tipping her out. She fell but stumbled, recovering, upright. All the stoner's placidness was gone now; he shoved at her, his strong hands at her back, yelling, 'Next,' as he forced her through a different door and Yolanda went sprawling, exactly as a sheep would totter down a slatted chute into the shocking light and shit and terror of the sheep yard, until she found herself in yet another room. Full of bald and frightened girls.

THE SECOND man, pale and pock-faced, is back in the room with Verla. He turns towards the door. When his hand is on the doorknob he glances back at her and says, 'Coming then?'

Her mouth is dry, she understands nothing. Even the girl led away seemed to understand, or else why say in that flat surly voice that she would go first? What did she know? After the girl let go of her hand, Verla's fingers flew to the windowsill; she must concentrate now to uncurl her grip.

Finally, some instinct rises. She runs her tongue over her teeth, furred like her mind. She hears her own thick voice deep inside her ears when she says, 'I need to know where I am.'

The man stands there, tall and narrow, hand still on the doorknob, surprised. He says, almost in sympathy, 'Oh, sweetie. You need to know *what* you are.'

And he draws from his pocket a slender little lead like the one he attached to the other girl. He steps back across the room towards Verla, and bends to clip the lead to the metal ring at her waist. She smells him: sour, like old milk.

'Come on,' he coaxes, as if she is a small dog, and gives a little tug on the leash. She lurches forwards, follows him outside.

On her blurred, faltering trot behind the man she tries to take in her surroundings. *Outback* is the first word that comes to her. Then *rubbish tip*. There are a few faded colourless fibro buildings, jagged black holes punched here and there in the panels. Roofs of mottled grey tin; crooked, hanging gutters. Narrow black slots of windows, paint peeling from frames. There are piles of corrugated-iron sheets and rotting timber, and old petrol drums on their sides. Tangles of wire. There is a rusted tractor, a jumble of metal pipes and prongs with dead white grass spiking through the gaps. No trees. And—she looks everywhere, quickly—other than the corroded, immovable tractor, no cars. No yellow bus.

They keep walking, the great hard leather boots—too big—scraping at her ankles.

'Hurry up,' he says, yanking the lead again. They pass a water tank on bricks with the disc of a lid leaning against it. Rust stains bleed from large ragged gouges in the side of the tank. The man jerks her along. 'Christ, you're slow,' he murmurs, as if she were an elderly animal he is leading. She is thirsty. In this hard sunlight with no trees nearby, the low-slung buildings—one, two, three that she can see, plus the one they have come from—offer no shade. There is a grassy dirt track, trailing off into the white haze beyond the buildings. Otherwise, only the flat white sky and the dusty ground.

It cannot be the outback, where Verla has never been. Has anyone? The outback is supposed to have red earth. This earth beneath her boots is not red. You could not even call it earth; just threadbare ground, grey gravel, dust.

She swelters in these stupid Amish clothes. She says, 'I'm thirsty.'

'Shut *up*,' says the man. He is bored with leading her around like a donkey. You can lead a horse to water but you cannot make it drink. *You can lead a whore to culture* was something said about her in the comments. Verla thinks of the empty water tank; a weird laugh begins rising up from her belly but dries up before it comes out.

Their feet crunch over a patch of stubbly dead grass, past a long concrete block—animal sheds, or disused toilets—then come upon another low pale weatherboard building. Up three rotting wooden steps to a narrow veranda. The man flings open an ancient flywire door so it bangs against the peeling weatherboards.

'Admissions,' he says. 'Come on.'

Inside is an airless makeshift office. A desk, a pin board stuck with curling bits of paper so old the printing has faded to nothing. He lets go of the lead and shoves Verla towards a green plastic outdoor chair, then sits down heavily in a torn vinyl office chair. He begins riffling through piles of handwritten pages on the desk. Verla tips her head back, breathing in the stifling air, and stares at the ceiling. Delicate webbed balloons of daddy-long-legs spiders dangle, wafting in the air.

The man suddenly snatches up an old-fashioned ink stamp and stamp pad, begins madly stamping. Verla does laugh this time, out loud. None of this can be happening.

The man stops stamping and looks at her patiently, bottom teeth combing his top lip. 'What's funny, Thirsty?'

'*Admissions!* Do you not even have laptops? What the fuck is this place?' Verla's voice is high and confused. The effect of the drugs has almost left her now, but for her terribly dry, dry mouth.

The man only returns to his crazed stamping, snorting a little laugh.

She persists. 'I need a glass of water, and then I need to make a phone call.'

The man sighs and stops rattling paper. It is as if he is in a play, and his job is to make the sound of paper rattling, and Verla has interrupted his performance. He pays stern, close attention to the page he has in his hand before putting it down and smiling. He leans over the table and talks to Verla in a horrible baby voice. 'Did you have your eyes shut on our little walk then, Thirsty? Why do you think I just *showed* you everything?'

Verla's chest constricts. 'I need to speak to my parents.' She does not say *parent*.

He is annoyed now. 'For fuck's sake, Princess. Do you see any phones? Computers? Phone towers outside?'

Disbelief rises in her. 'No,' she says. She means, *I refuse*. At last she is enraged, shoots to her feet to roar—for it is, finally, intolerable, this stupid, stupid game, performance, this *bullshit*—but the man steps nimbly around the table and in an instant plants his big black boot in her stomach so hard she is slammed back against the wall.

While Verla curls, weeping, on the dusty floor, Boncer returns to his desk and his rattling papers.

'WHO ARE you, the village idiot?'

There they were, in the middle of that day in their thick scratchy costumes, standing in a clump on the gravel. Ten girls, all their heads newly shaved (Yolanda felt again the cold snap of scissor blades near her ears, the hair landing in her lap like moths). All wore the same strange prairie workhouse tunic, the oat-coloured calico blouse. The rock-hard leather boots and coarse knitted socks, like out of some hillbilly TV show from the eighties. Or even older.

Yolanda stood thinking of the two stars she had seen in the night. Enormous headlights in the sky; one, as big as her fingertip, *moving*. Was this possible? In her drugged mind, she had thought it a spaceship come to save her.

The skinny man asked again if she was the village idiot, stepping up to stare right into her face. He was not much older than the oldest girl here—maybe twenty-five? The flaky skin on his long flat face was marked here and there with old acne scars. Now he was so close to her, Yolanda could see on his chin, just below the right corner of his mouth, the swell of a blind pimple beginning.

Already she knew better than to answer him.

He muttered to the ground for them to get in line. As he waited for them to shuffle into formation he pursed his lips sideways, gingerly pressing a fingertip to the rising pimple, and wincing.

One big girl, fair-skinned with fleshy cheeks and wide, swimmer's shoulders, said irritably, 'What? We can't *hear* you,' and then closed her eyes against the sun, hands on her hips, murmuring something beneath her breath. So she didn't see the man's swift, balletic leap—impossibly pretty and light across the gravel—and a leather-covered baton in his hand coming *whack* over the side of her jaw. They all cried out with her as she fell, shrieking in pain. Some of their arms came out to try to catch her. They cowered. More than one began crying as they hurried then, into a line.

The man Boncer cast an aggrieved look at them, as if they were to blame for the stick in his hand, then sighed. The big-cheeked girl rocked on her haunches and moaned, arms swaddling her head and jaw, which surely must be broken from the force of the belting. Yolanda waited for Boncer to move towards her, to send for first aid. To look worried. But he only stood fingering his pimple, until the girls either side of the beaten girl gently took her elbows and raised her to stand.

'Now: march,' Boncer said, petulant. Turning his brown leather stick in his hands, its hard, lumpily stitched seams like a botched wound. Like a scar that would make worse ones.

They stared at him in panic.

But another girl next to Yolanda, forehead shining with sweat, her gaze on the stick, began to swing her arms, marching on the spot. She knew what to do. As if she were leading a bunch of soldiers, not girls. Out of her small body came a scrawny little voice, crying: '*Left*, left, left-right-*left*.' Leading a—a battalion, her arms swinging high.

'Ooh, yes!' cried Boncer, skipping to her side. 'That's the way, ladies! Follow the army slut! You next, village idiot!' He leaped along the line, clipping the girls' leashes one to the other, then scurried to the front. He too began swinging his arms high and stomping out the rhythm, crying out *left-right-left* and leading the straggling line of beaten girls in their olden-day clothes out across the paddocks under the broiling white sun.

This, Yolanda knew, was true madness: she was entering it with these new sisters as sure with quiet awe as back in her childhood when she and Darren, seven and five, would step inside the cool dark of a beach cave at the end of the white sand when their mother took them to the sea each year.

Left-right-left.

Yolanda and Darren, stepping with their soft bare feet over the cold sea-washed pebbles into the watery cave, rippling half with fear and half with wonder.

• • •

The girls marched for two hours.

Yolanda held down panic by casting back through the years. She counted houses, schools, boyfriends, counted the years back to childhood again, till she reached the old flat in Seymour Road. Revisited her mother's boxes of wax lining the musty hallway; other people's hairs in the bathtub. The squashy green velvet couch piled at one end with the faded pink towels speckled with white bleach splotches. In their mother's room, under the bed, the heavy porridge-coloured folding massage table that Gail would drag out into the lounge and snap into shape whenever she had a client.

The children never knew how she knew when a client

would arrive, but Gail would say, 'I've got Mrs Goldman coming at three,' or, 'Wendy Pung will be here in a minute,' and the children would shift off their perches in the nests of the folded towels, and go into the bathroom to switch on the kettle, and then sit cross-legged on the floor to watch television while their mother ushered another thick-legged woman into the flat. Their childhood was the buttery smell of wax, the sound of sharp little rips and hissing breath as their mother tugged lumps of wax away and the women quietly gasped. Gail's hands were smooth and cool and she patted and murmured over the women's white skin, pulling their underwear this way and that. It was Yolanda's job afterwards to melt the gobs of wax in the little battered aluminium pot on the electric stove, to fish out and throw away the cotton strips and to sieve the hot wax through the pantyhose into the big tin. ('Of course it's clean!' her mother cried with fury, hands on her hips, at the health inspector that time, before she got the fine for running an illegal business.) All the coarse black hairs and the pale fine ones too, caught there in the stocking mesh.

• • •

Her boots began to scrape painfully at her heels through the damp socks. The only sound was the girls' heavy, frightened panting as they marched, the trudge of their boots over the stony ground. And the fine, light tinkle of the leash-fasteners against the metal rings.

• • •

Sometimes her mother's clients would lie on the table face up, their eyes closed and hands folded across their bellies while Gail basted their faces with custardy lotions, pressed wet cotton balls over their eyelids. Sometimes the women would chatter while Gail worked: about real estate, businesses that were closing, about their errant sons, the hospitalisations of their friends. Their voices were a pleasant purr beneath the cartoon soundtrack on television. Or sometimes the women would lie on their softly spreading bellies in their underwear while Yolanda's mother massaged them, rolling the thick white flesh of their backs and thighs under her hands, working back and forth over their bodies, kneading flesh. These times Yolanda and Darren would lean backwards, silently, on their haunches to look at the woman's face squashed into the padded oval hole of the massage table. The women's eyes were always shut and their faces were flattened and stretched by the pressure of the surface, mouths wide and lips flat against their teeth, and they looked like those photos of the faces of astronauts going into space. Yolanda and Darren would smile slyly at each other as sometimes the women dribbled and made small grunting sounds as their mother worked away at them above. Occasionally one would fall asleep and begin to snore lightly, and those times even Gail would smile with the children.

When they were leaving at the end, almost every time, the women would glance across the room and then whisper to Gail, *That girl of yours, my god.* Sometimes it was people in the street who stopped and said, *What a beauty.* Made jokes about touches of the tar brush and how exotic and *when she's a teen* and locks and keys and boys.

When the women had gone, the massage table was Spray-and-Wiped and folded away, slid under Gail's bed once again, and towels were washed and the grumbling of the tumble dryer began in the bathroom, filling the flat with sweet-smelling, moist warm air.

• • •

The walking was harder now the track had run out; the line moved slower as they scrambled awkwardly up the hillside, ascending the slope in their slippery leather boots that could not grip. The path that had been not even a track really, just pale flattened grass, had turned fainter and disappeared after the first half-hour or so. Boncer stopped now and then, squinting into the sun, looking east and west, then turning back to cast the girls a surly, contemptuous look before moving ahead. Did even he know where they were going?

• • •

The people in the next-door flat were German, with an Australian flag on a proper flagpole sticking out from their balcony. They complained to each other in thick accents about the smell from Darren's mice, which lived on Yolanda's mother's balcony in a birdcage. The mice did smell: sourly nutty and musty. Every few weeks more mice would be born, and the floor of the cage became a slithering mound of dusky pink thumbs, hairless and menacing with their rawness and need. When the babies were ten days old (their hair so fine you wanted to hold them against your closed eyelid, but they squirmed and stank), Darren would scoop them up with the dustpan, drop them into a bucket and carry them down the stairs. At the back of the block of flats, up near the privet behind the laundry block, he would tip them tumbling out of the bucket and watch them run blindly in all directions. The mama mouse and the two big fat black ones barely seemed to notice that the babies had gone. The fat ones sniffed around the edges of the cage.

She supposed they were the fathers of the babies that never stopped coming.

Yolanda feared that mother mouse and her cold, incessant production. It was something to do with her, she knew, not Darren. It had something to do with the hairlessness of the women on Gail's bench, the squirming babies, with all the creams and lotions, with their whispering to her mother, *What a beauty*, but meaning something adult and uneasy and expectant.

And it was to do with this place, Yolanda knew; with her presence here in this line of bewildered, trudging girls. Some limped heavily now as they jerked and stumbled along, chained together like prisoners. They were prisoners.

TWO HOURS of marching, the girls snivelling softly and their feet bleeding into their socks. Verla, last in the line, watches them hobbling up the slope before her, their arms no longer swinging in marching time—except when this Boncer turns around now and then to scowl at them—but flailing in an effort to keep their balance as they scramble up the pale tussocky hill.

Boncer is hot; his blue overalls show dark sweat patches at his armpits and in a blurred crucifix down his narrow back. But the girls, in their calico and canvas clothes and buckles and rough woollen socks and hard boots with leather soles that slip and slide over the shiny dead grass, are hotter. Some girls have unhooked the bibs of their tunics so the flaps fall open down their fronts, but this makes it more difficult to walk. They must clutch at the waists of the dresses to hold them up. All of them have rolled up the rasping calico sleeves, exposing the skin of their forearms. When Verla glances up, instead of down at her feet and at the uneven ground meeting each step and threatening her ankles, she sees that all their necks and their raw naked scalps are burning.

The land, which she first thought so flat, is in fact a wide shallow dish. Its lip forms a ridge, and as she looks around she sees it encircles the whole compound. It is one side of this dish they are climbing now, towards the trickle of scrub and bush creeping down the ridge to their left—with the sun so high it's impossible to tell if it is east or west or what. But apart from this surging tide of bush, the bowl of land seems scraped and bare.

When Boncer turns around, wheezing, his face is red to the roots of his greasy black hair and his upper lip shines with moisture. He does not look well. He turns back and trudges along at the head of the line, too tired now, it seems, to raise his stick or command them to straighten up or swing their arms *higher* as he did in the beginning.

Where are they? One girl now and then lurches around and mouths this question to the girl behind: *Where are we going?*

Verla's mind fills with gruesome images from her studies, from global atrocities and wars, from snatched memories of news footage, blurry mobile phone pictures. Lines of men and boys marched to open graves and shot at the edge, falling in so nobody has to tire themselves moving bodies. No women in these lines; they are kept for other purposes. Verla's bowels convulse. Yet Boncer has no weapon but his stick—or perhaps he does; she peers at the flapping fabric of his overalls, searching his body for a gun. It is impossible to tell—how would she, whose knowledge of crime comes from television and precise essays on international law, or more mundanely from the sad men and women her mother visits in prison, detect a pistol? How would she recognise it, or know what to do with it? It is ludicrous.

What would happen if they refused to walk? He could beat one of them, but together they could overpower him. She assesses the line of drugged and weakened girls. Why have they been so stupid as to follow him? Why this trailing, limping obedience?

They walk on, strung together with the little leads. The sun rises higher.

The land moves beneath their feet, and the little clutch of buildings slides further and further behind them, until when Verla glances back it has become just a small swatch, a few messy angular brushstrokes of white on the scrappy brown land.

As she marches, Verla carries other selves inside her.

There is the terrified girl who feels the swollen, tender pain of her kicked stomach and bruised shoulder from this morning, who feels the skin of her heels slipping off in shreds. But who is already understanding with dull surprise that some pain is endurable, as the hard rims of her boots rub through the rough wool, sponging and scouring the skin away, and is discovering that she can breathe and breathe and keep on walking.

There is another self, who stops walking and says, calm and commanding, *Oh, enough. Let's go home*, to whom the man Boncer turns and weeps with relief, taking her soft white hand in his as they scramble back down the hill to a line of waiting cars that drive them home all through the day and the night.

There is another Verla, who whispers a plan to the other girls through the line, and they round on Boncer, stove in his head with stones and make their way home, leaving his forlorn, pulpy body to the dingoes.

And longest, most desperately, there is true Verla, one warm evening lying back on her elbows on the velvety boards of the small harbour jetty while her father fishes, the taut silver thread of fishing line triangulating the water, the blue evening sky, her father in his chair, the pole in his good hand. This self admires her own long legs stretched out over the wooden boards before her, the elegance of her ankles and toes. She feels her body pulse in its ease and smoothness, her own abundant youth, while she smokes a cigarette and her father frowns down at her but cannot speak and she promises, *It's okay, Dad, I'm only having one*, and knows her mother to be at home scrolling through her emails and resentfully peeling prawns, and when her phone buzzes lowly beside her, turning its slow circle on the jetty boards, this Verla answers it softly and says, *Okay, yes, we're ready*, and then reels in the line and gathers up the fishing things. And tucks her father's feet neatly into place and turns the wheelchair for home.

But this pure Verla is unreachably in the past. Before honours year and internship, before that European trip and her unravelling by poetry and paintings and politics. Before Andrew.

As the procession climbs the nubbled grey ridge, the high dry air begins to vibrate in waves, shrilling louder as they march. Cicadas. Verla remembers prep school Bible glimpses: plagues of locusts, punishments from the skies. She looks up now, expecting a teeming cloud, but the sky is still cloudless, white with heat. Soon they cannot hear anything, not the powdery trudge of their steps on the earth, not the tinkle of the leash-fasteners, only the screaming insects, filling all their eyes and ears and nostrils and pores with that acid warping of the air.

Verla keeps her eyes on the girl in front of her. Now and then the calico shirt slips and Verla can see the smudged edge of a tattoo on her shoulder: gaudy pink, a sickly orange, a thick dark outline like stained glass. She cannot make out the picture.

After a while she hears rhythms in the insects' noise. Pulses, exhalations, as though the bush is breathing. *You need to know what you are*, this Boncer had said to her. In the cicadas' rhythmic shrilling the words hover, almost visible, in the air. The words and the cicada noise become Verla's own pulse trying to answer, every nerve in her responding to this membrane of noise pressing in. She cannot know where she is, or why, and yet something in her knows her survival depends on this electric white question. *What am I?*

The cicadas are deafening now, warning. The girls struggle up the ridge and soon are walking among small slender trees, sweating with effort. Then a straight line distinguishes itself between the rippling trunks: a soaring metal fence and, beyond it, a dirty sea of scrub. On this side of the fence are the leaning scrappy trees, the scuffed earth dotted with low scrubby bushes that scratch at their calves as they walk. On the other side, pressing in, the thick unknowable bush.

Boncer stops walking. He turns to face them at the head of the line, wipes his face with his sleeve. He yanks hard on the leash so they make a little stumbling caterpillar, until he has them bunched together.

They stare at the fence, and see it is in fact a huge black gate. On its other side, very faint, a sort of track is discernible between the trees, though nothing you could call a road. More a vague, wide path through the shrubs and broken-off twigs, the track soon disappearing among the bushes. *Fire trail* is the term that comes to Verla, though how she knows it she has no idea.

A low hum can be heard inside the cicadas' wall of noise. Already, against their weird colonial clothes, the fence seems futuristic, fantastical. The gate has no hinges that Verla can see, no visible padlock or latch. It would have to slide. Its anodised black poles match those of the rest of the fence, reaching into the vast air, at least two storeys high, and angling back towards them at the top. Every few centimetres, from the ground upwards, is a taut strand of new barbed wire, secured to the post spine with a thick black plastic knob. At the top, where the poles change angle, a large coil of thicker barbed wire runs the length of the fence, as far as Verla can see, in both directions. Every twenty metres or so rises another stern pole, studded from bottom to top with the beetle-black knobs.

Still, Verla thinks, her heart thudding, *I could climb that.*

Then she understands that the wires are humming. It is this bass note lying beneath the cicadas' shimmering noise.

With the other girls, Verla stares at the knobbled poles, but what comes to her now are visions not of electrocution but of church spires in Barcelona, crusted and castellated, crenellated with knobbles against the high blue sky. When Andrew took her on his infrastructure and transport tour, they visited churches. It was not Andrew's art history lectures or the poetry that came out later, of course, not the gore of crucifixions, the holy agony and the thorns and blood; all the media cared about was hotel bills and cocktail prices. The Verla of that trip was nonplussed in the face of all that Spanish slaughter and violence, for what could she, ripe with willingness, with risk, with being *chosen*, ever have known of suffering?

Now, she will know pain. Staring up at these lethal humming spires, Verla feels it, in a great tidal sweep. She wants to get down on her knees, beat her head on the stony earth, she wants to roll in ashes and cry out, *I understand.*

There is a yank on the lead, and Boncer is shouting to be heard over the cicadas' cries and the fence. 'Six metres high. If you try to climb through and your head or neck touches an electric wire—they are all electric—you will be rendered unconscious, and if you fall unconscious on the wires you will receive multiple shocks over a period of minutes to hours and in this case your heart will stop and you will die. This event happens quickly. The fence is electrified afresh every zero point seven kilometres.'

So Boncer recites, their disillusioned tour guide, picking delicately with his thumbnail at a flake of skin at the edge of his nostril as he speaks. He looks past the girls as he lists amp figures and voltages, then trails off, distracted by something far off in the distance. The girls follow his gaze along the fence line. Every so often they can make out the hump of something—a rotting animal—at its base. Here and there on the fence itself is the black flapping rag of a burnt bird or bat.

'Look over there,' Boncer orders. They shuffle, turn in the opposite direction. They squint along the ridge, following his pointing finger. Can see nothing but haze of heat wobble, some far, far distant hills. But all the way round, the faint, sketched thread of the fence is visible. 'The electric fence travels the entire ridge, all the way around the station,' Boncer shouts.

The girls lick their lips, shading their eyes. They can barely stand now. Most are bent forwards, hands on their knees, nodding at the ground. The girl who was hit stands breathing carefully with her eyes closed, cupping her swelling jaw with two hands, tears sliding down over her wrists.

'Time to go back,' Boncer shouts over the cicadas. Then casually, but so fast—how does he possess such speed?—he grabs the shoulders of the nearest girl in the line and shoves her hard so she overbalances, one forearm forced to the fence wire. Her arm jerks wildly and now she is on the tussocks, shrieking and curling in pain, the others yanked to the ground after her, beads on a string. The girl with the broken jaw bellows as she, too, falls.

'Well,' yells Boncer, 'some of you slags might not of *believed* me.' Again the aggrieved, sulky face.

Suddenly the cicadas stop. Boncer looks through the fence at the wall of scrub. They all do. The only sound now is the ticking bush, a trilling bird somewhere, the humming fence, the panting and moans of the injured girls.

'Get up.'

He moves along the line, checking the little locks on the leads—Verla can smell his sweat—and then unclips and reattaches himself, this time to a ring at Verla's back, so he is now last in line.

He marches them all the way down the hillside. Every now and then he jabs at Verla's spine with the leather stick, and during the next hours—everyone is slower descending than climbing—he reaches past her twice to thwack at the ears of two girls he thinks have spoken. But it is only the hot, empty wind.

• • •

It is almost sunset when they reach the buildings again. They limp in the dust. Some of the compound is familiar to Verla from this morning, now the sedation has worn off. The buildings are not on level ground after all, but the gradual start of the land's rise. The flat is beyond, down in the paddocks, where she can see a patch of murky brown water: a near-empty dam. They pass the office. The long shed she thought was concrete but now sees is unpainted fibro, grey and brittle. Some of the walls have been patched, like the flat eave-less roof, with corrugated iron. There are other buildings too, ones she did not notice before. All look abandoned, except by vermin.

'March,' says Boncer, but hoarsely. He too is weary. They are nearing the largest building. Verla thinks it is the place she first came to consciousness all those years ago this morning, in the room the other girl entered.

'Teddy,' calls out Boncer, in half-hearted greeting. And there, waiting on the veranda, leaning against the post in his blue overalls, hands in his pockets, is the younger man with the dreadlocks, the head-shaver. As the line of girls scuffs towards the steps he turns to go inside, holding the screen door open for the first in line, but not looking at them. He stares instead at the floor.

Inside it is cool and dark. The girls sigh in relief at this welcome gloom, shuffling along after Teddy on their leads through rooms and corridors. It is some kind of house. There are mantelpieces and faded curtains at the windows, and tables, and even bookshelves—empty. Teddy leads them on, through the maze of tacked-on room after room. There is a large blank sitting room, with four torn red vinyl couches, bulging and sagging, and nothing else but an ancient bulbous television in the corner, unplugged. Through another door, along another narrow corridor, lined with closed doors. Bedrooms, surely. Verla almost sinks to her knees with longing at the thought of a bed, any bed. But on they march. She waits for the room in which she woke, but it does not come. Then suddenly Teddy stops. They are in a broad, light room with dirty floral curtains at a window, an ugly painted mantelpiece, a long wooden table with a white melamine surface. Pine benches line each side of the table.

Teddy moves along the row of girls, unclipping the leads. From one, a whispered question: 'Can we sit down, please?', and he shrugs. They fall, their legs buckling, to the benches.

There is nothing on the table. They slump over the white surface, faces buried in their folded arms. There will be no washing of hands or faces, no changing of dust-crusted, bloody socks, no water. The big girl with the broken jaw sits straight-backed, still cupping her face with one hand, as she has done all day. For the first several hours she whimpered and softly cried. Now she makes no sound; her lips are grey. The side of her face—jaw, cheek, eye—has ballooned and the skin appears to be tightening painfully. Across the table from Verla, the girl who Boncer pushed onto the fence lies with her face on the table, cradling her burnt arm in her lap.

It is not over.

'You three—up,' says Teddy, prodding the three girls nearest him.

They drag themselves up, limp after him through a door, turning at the last second to cast terrified glances at the rest. Verla can only sink deeper with relief at being left, lays down her head, closes her eyes. Boncer has disappeared. Nobody speaks. In a moment Verla will—must—learn things, but just now she is too exhausted. Her blisters bleed into her socks, but her feet are mercifully still.

She is roused by the clunk of crockery near her head. Shallow thick white ceramic bowls and white enamel cups are dropped in front of each place by the first girl who followed Teddy out. Verla sits up, and sees the second servant girl walking carefully, a large battered aluminium saucepan heavy in her hands. Behind her is the third girl, with a ladle. They proceed along the table, ladling some unidentifiable, bright yellow slop into the bowls.

Teddy reappears with two jugs of water and moves along behind the girls, sloshing water into the enamel cups. Every girl seizes her cup, sucking and slurping. A look of sympathy flashes across Teddy's face, but he recovers. He fills the cups again and says, 'After this it's bore water. Unless it rains.'

Verla feels the room contract with fear: Boncer is back. He drops a handful of spoons on the table. Girls' hands dart and snatch, and then Teddy says, 'Well, *eat*,' and they lunge at their dishes like dogs.

Verla gobbles with the rest, at whatever this muck is. Later, she learns it is supposed to be macaroni cheese, powdered, from a packet. For now she does not care, spooning the sandy yellow stuff into her mouth, swallowing, spooning again. The only sound is scraping cutlery on china. The artificial cheese leaves a lurid, watery residue in the bowl. She has to resist an urge to lick it. She feels strength flicker, then fall away again. She sits staring at the empty bowl and the enamel cup before her. She notices now that the bowls are printed with curving pale blue text around the rims. HARDINGS INTERNATIONAL, Verla reads. DIGNITY & RESPECT IN A SAFE & SECURE ENVIRONMENT. The bowls around her are scraped with spoons and the girls breathe through their mouths like animals.

You need to know what you are. Verla is not an animal. She looks up from her bowl, around at the blank faces of these other girls. Sallow, fat, thin, red-eyed, dark-circled. Pink-skinned, thick-lipped, foreheads shiny or grazed with fine pimples. Their shaved heads the pink of raw sausage—or dirty, dark, like the shadows in armpits. Misshapen, all. Strange what shapes a skull could be, how much ugliness is hidden by hair. Some have little scabs of dried blood where the razor has nicked them.

She herself has been brought here unlawfully.

Verla knows they will all say that. But knows herself, too, as separate from—beyond—the rest of them. She will be released from here.

Then, directly at the other end of the table, she sees the girl from the room this morning. Staring back at Verla, meeting her gaze, expressionless. Did they hold hands, filled with terror? Had they spoken? Or is this some memory from childhood, sent through dreams to flicker and furnish Verla's drug-fucked mind?

They stare, the two of them, and Verla realises with a cold, slow shock that the face she stares into belongs to Yolanda Kovacs.

Verla is not a child nor a prostitute nor a ward of the state whose parents have abused or abandoned her. She is a parliamentary intern, a rightful citizen, and she cannot be held in this place. But—Yolanda Kovacs is also a citizen by law, whatever sex she did or did not consent to with however many footballers, and here she sits with her heavy-lidded eyes and her famous mouth and unabashed stare, looking more fearsome now, more handsome than she ever did in any of the TV footage or the magazines or the newspaper front pages.

Verla looks around the table then. Despite the shaven skulls, one by one the girls' faces clarify for an instant—and then merge, and Verla knows that she and they are in some dreadful way connected.

Boncer's words return. In the days to come she will learn *what she is*, what they all are. That they are the minister's-little-travel-tramp and that-Skype-slut and the yuck-ugly-dog from the cruise ship; they are pig-on-a-spit and big-red-box, moll-number-twelve and bogan-gold-digger-gangbang-slut. They are what happens when you don't keep your fucking fat slag's mouth shut.

POXY BONNET on its hook.

Even from the bed as she looked at it hanging there, Yolanda could feel its greasy, clammy weight. Its long beak pointing floorwards. And the fucking thing stank.

Soon the beating on the doors would come and she would get out of the bed and dress in the other rank things: tunic, smock thing, whatever. The musty underclothes and socks, unwashed since they first arrived. Then she would take the bonnet from the hook and fit it to her grubby bald head.

The visor of the bonnet was rounded, a long half-tunnel you looked down. When you had it on it was like playing blind man's bluff, like wearing a periscope, you couldn't see anything but a small round patch before you. If you wanted to talk to someone you had to swing your head right around and then all you saw was the side of their beak. It was clever, really. Even when you got up the guts to talk, it put you off.

Until the door-bashing came, Yolanda would lie on the bed and wait. From the sounds and the gloomy light, it was still very early.

She was used to the noises now; after three days, they all were. The ticks and cracks of the corrugated-iron sheets heating up and cooling, and the noises of the other girls in the night, their cries and calls. Sometimes, their lonely rhythmic breath. After that first day's marching, then the food (so-called), they had been driven down here like dogs—Teddy this time, with a thick sharp stick he just picked off the ground—to what he called the shearers' quarters. He yelled it, a command: 'Get! Shearers' quarters!' They just stood there because they didn't know what the fuck he was talking about, and that was when he started whacking the long stick on the ground. Turned out it made sense to herd them like dogs, because shearers' quarters was what Yolanda had already seen and thought were kennels. They all did. That Verla especially went off, yelping and flailing and screeching, *You will not put us in that box*, so she was first in when Teddy did put them in there. He clipped them to a post outside in their shitty little chain gang, and then unlocked the padlock for each girl one by one, dragged her along the corridor, gripping by the upper arm—which *hurt*; he looked like a skinny feral but it turned out he was strong—and shoved them in through a door and bolted it shut after.

Yolanda waited in line outside, taking in the corrugated-tin walls, the tiny window slots and thinking, *I never knew shearers got kept like dogs.* It didn't matter, though; they'd all be dead by morning.

But once you were inside you realised you'd been here already, that you'd woken up here that morning off your face, and so you went straight to the little slot of a window and sucked air into your mouth, and you didn't suffocate after all.

You heard things at night, padding around outside. Dogs maybe, maybe dingoes, maybe Boncer and Teddy, maybe that woman Yolanda thought she heard at the head-shaving the first day but had never seen since. Did she exist, and where?

You heard light footfalls in the dead grass, could be leaves or a plastic bag they were treading on. Could be someone eating their lunch from a paper bag, sitting out there having a picnic in the dark, in the baking soundless grounds of a girls' prison made out of shearers' kennels in the middle of fucking nowhere.

Yolanda had heard them most nights. Someone walking around, creeping, while she lay in an old steel bed with a rippling tin door locked and bolted.

Sometimes she got up and went to her window again, like that first night, to look for the two stars. That was when she heard the bird noises. In her dreaming mind these grew together, the bonnets and the girls with their weeping night-bird noises, and she became aware, convinced, that the bonnet beaks were made of bird bones. Cartilage from wings, from the spines of feathers, woven together or fused somehow under heat. They wore the bones of dead birds, and the night cries of birds and girls too were put to use.

Sometimes Yolanda thought she *was* going mad, but maybe it was the drugs still. She wished she had them again now, the ones that made you forget. The ones dentists used, and abortionists.

There were no mirrors here. Strange, but she could almost forget her body, that marvellous thing. She used to stand before the mirror, wondering at it. It was something, all right. Must be, to cause such fuss. She would stand there staring at it, trying to understand, to see it as they saw it. Filling her hands with the bosoms, cradling the soft belly. Parting herself gently for a moment with her fingers. V for victory. That was a joke, any rate.

Was it the softness, perhaps, that made them want it so much? And hate it so much? The body was separate from her, it was a thing she wore. The things that were done to it had nothing to do with her, Yolanda, at all.

But afterwards she was told it wasn't the body, it was her own desire. What did she think she was there for, a cuppa Milo? She was *up for it one hundred percent*, all that jazz. But how could she be, she wanted to scream at them, when she wasn't even there? She had floated out from herself, and away. She wasn't even there. Still wasn't, when she let that night come back to her.

So now she lay on the bed and waited, which was kind of funny because doing that was what had started all this. But nothing could be more different, because here was the rasping nightgown even in the heat, the vast empty land outside coming alive and nobody caring where she was, even her troublesome body forgotten except for this: to march, to feel pain, to hunger and thirst, to eat and to sleep, to piss and shit and bleed.

IN THE black night Verla wakes underwater. This submarine tinks and cracks with the great pressure of the surrounding water, above and below, at the thin skin of the vessel. Soon she will be hurled, engulfed by the ocean exploding inwards. She will be torn to pieces, and the only living part of her drowned.

She lies panting in the hot air, smelling the night. Heart beating hard. Something is out there again, trudging and stopping, something tearing at the roots of the dry grass beyond this box. The corrugated iron bangs and creaks. Her heart slows, and she is submerged once more.

Before dawn she wakes again with the birds. Kookaburras, cockatoos, somewhere far off. Her back aches, she needs desperately to piss. Light seams the door and the window slot, cracks between the iron panels, softly at first, then in sharp bright lines. The room . . . it is not a room—what is it? A shed, a stall for animals. A kennel with a dirty wooden floor and corrugated-iron walls battened with wood. A kennel big enough to stand up in, to contain a single iron-framed bed.

The gloom slowly dissolves, the morning grows lighter. She lies on the bony mattress. The disinfectant smell is still here, but fading with each day. She counts the tin panels again, six squares made by the wooden battens on each wall. The different colours of the grey iron, smeared and darkened in patches, with what? Oil, grease? Blood?

On a nail banged into one of the battens is the uniform, already stinking of her body from the heat. And the vile bonnet. Beneath the bed, the tangle of hospital-blue plastic that she supposed had contained the worn floral sheets, the flat stained pillow, that first day. That afternoon they were shoved in here and the doors padlocked behind them and they sat on the hard beds with the faded sheets and thought they would die in the night, and later wished they had.

She will keep the plastic, useful for when it becomes finally unbearable. She does not want to think of how much less bearable it could get. She imagines the plastic over her face, her eyes pressed closed.

The tin walls are heating up already, blowflies dotting against them, their arrhythmic drones making it feel even hotter than it is. The clatter of dishes comes from up at the house, sound carrying easily on the still morning air.

Her room (not room: cell, *dogbox*) is at the end of the row. She can hear the girls in the adjoining boxes; next to her is Isobel Askell the airline girl, then Hetty the cardinal's girl with the burnt and ulcerating arm, then Yolanda Kovacs, then the rest: Maitlynd the school principal's '*head* girl'; then big Barbs; and next that morose gamer girl Rhiannon, the one called Codebabe and the wanking mascot for every nasty little gamer creep in the country. Then poor cruise-ship Lydia, then Leandra from the army, then last of all, the girl the whole country could despise: little Asian Joy, from last season's *PerforMAXX*. Who got fat, then thin after everything happened, and who could barely speak a word now, let alone sing one.

She hears Izzy shifting on the squeaking metal bed, sighing into her sweaty rosebud sheets in the dawn.

Verla gets out of bed, her bladder stinging now intolerably, and not for the first time steps to the corner furthest from the adjoining cell, squats and pisses onto the dusty wooden boards as quietly as she can. She chooses a spot with the widest gaps between the boards.

They sometimes call out to one another. On the first morning their small voices were heard, muffled, passing from one dogbox to the next—*hello?*—and they learned that none of them had died in the night. Since then they have passed their stories to one another through the thin tin walls. For these first days there is only one story: the last thing they remember of their lives, the moment before they dropped into that dark molasses, that dragging down. The moment they were put under and handed over. The stories are different, the times and places—*I was at the doctor's*; *I was in a club with my sister*; *I think I was in a taxi*—but the shame is shared, that none of them saw how they were being handed over. How foolishly lured and tricked.

Despite her own shame, Verla feels sorry for the rest of the girls: nobody will look for them. When his staff's treachery is discovered and Andrew gets her out, when she is released (not *rescued*, that word for stupid princesses and children), she will advocate for these girls. When Georgie fucking Mullan is excommunicated and Verla reinstated, compensated. It cannot take much longer. Verla was seen in that restaurant with Mullan and her falsehoods, people saw them, it will be all over the media by now.

Verla straightens, steps away from the shameful little puddle. She knows her pissing can be heard by Izzy and more of the girls, possibly even smelled, but nobody says anything through the walls. She knows that she will be able to forget this when she is back home.

She clambers back into the bed to wait for the beating on the doors. Outside a sweep of cockatoos passes overhead, screaming.

Sometimes she hears weeping echoing along the boxes. Sometimes a muttering, like begging or prayer.

It's not only the girls Verla hears.

Boncer and Teddy sit in two rotting, sagging cane chairs beneath her window outside the dogboxes at night. First it was to stop the girls calling out to each other at night—Boncer raining thundering smashes on the tin with his stick if he heard the slightest noise, even though the girls mostly fall instantly asleep from exhaustion. Now, each night, the two men simply sit, muttering and smoking. Boncer interrogates Teddy: *Are you a faggot?* And when Teddy sighs and says mildly, *No, mate, I'm not, but I don't think you should be using that word*, Boncer merely titters, *You so are, a fucking hippie faggot.*

Teddy has been backpacking, Verla learns. On his way across to the coast (what coast? She strains and strains to hear, but he never says where to or from), he took this gig for some fast cash—the mines had nothing for him—before six months of diving trips. When Hardings comes he's off again.

Each night, leaden with tiredness and pain—the span of it across her shoulders and neck from carrying concrete guttering all day, the sharp stabs in her stomach still from Boncer's kicking the first day, the bloody blisters stinging anew every time she peels off the filthy socks, taking with them a layer of new skin—Verla has ground her teeth and tried to stay awake, to make sense of these fragments. Mines, diving coast, when Hardings comes.

Yolanda and some of the others have spoken of a woman here somewhere, but she is never mentioned by the men. Verla has learned nothing from her listening, understands little but their low murmurs about girls they have fucked—Teddy says *made love*, but Boncer doesn't, and calls Teddy a faggot again. She freezes in her hard iron bed the first time she hears the word *girls*, and then Teddy says it's good they can't fuck these ones, because of the bonuses and that, but also who wants sloppy seconds anyway? *You'd feel sort of soiled after*, he says, and Boncer, after a pause, agrees. *Definite sluts*, he adds. Then, a moment later, *But if you did, which one would you?* Teddy says nothing, thinking, and then says, *Nah*. There's another pause, and, *Think of the bonuses, mate*. Verla hears a slap at a mosquito on skin, Boncer saying *fuck off* softly into the night air. Then Teddy musing, *We'll have to watch ourselfs down the track though, I s'pose.*

Verla knows then what could be worse than now.

TEDDY PERCHES in his usual spot on the veranda rail as Boncer leads them up the hill, still clipped together in their flimsy chain gang, to go back to the room where they eat. On the first day Boncer announced it as The Refectory, as if this place is an actual institution instead of a nightmare, as if the musty little room with its pitted table and faded curtains and mantelpiece has some sort of status, as if any of this is justifiable. Now he calls it the re*fuck*tory, sniggering every time.

All the girls are mottled with bruises now after six days of Boncer's stick. The bruises flower yellow and purple over their arms, legs, their backs and thighs and breastbones under the coarse tunics. They move like old peasant women, hobbling, trying to march as ordered, the ragged line of them limping and lurching in the morning sun.

Verla aches too, and watches from the shadow beneath her bonnet's beak as Teddy comes back into view, sunning himself, content, lizardy—eyes closed, face tilted to the sun—in the crook of rail and post. One leg lying along the rail, smooth bare foot extended, the other anchored to the boards.

He opens his eyes and moves only his head to watch them as they march up the steps below him, surveying their parade with a benign curiosity, as if it's a trail of ducks or goats he's following with his sleepy gaze. At last he swings languidly down from the railing and stands on his elegant feet, flexes his long spine, rolls his shoulders. Like some yoga teacher on retreat, stretching and preening and saluting the sun. As Verla nears him, last in line, he lifts the thick seaweedy coils of his dreadlocks up behind his head, twisting them into a turban, his tall wobbling crown. Verla hears him following them into the dark house. A few blowflies, sinking in the heavy air, sail into the gloom, and the flyscreen slowly bangs to a close behind them.

At the table Verla considers the curdling powdered milk in her bowl, turns her face from it so as not to gag, her bonnet pointing. The bowls have not been washed since the first day, and a hardened layer of translucent yellow stuff coats the ceramic beneath the ragged orange flakes and the sour milk. She cannot eat it, but she must. Boncer stands leaning against the wall, heavy keys dangling from his belt, one boot toe resting on the floor. He stares through the open window at Teddy, who, his dishing-out duties done (the pile of filthy bowls flung onto the table), has once again taken up residence on the railing and now meticulously bites his fingernails. Pruning and nipping, working his way along the fine fingers of one hand, then the other.

It's not just Boncer watching Teddy; they all do. Teddy has the golden skin of a surfer, a busker. A delicate face. How old is he? Nineteen? Twenty-four? Beneath his Adam's apple, inside the rough blue fabric of the boiler suit, a fine plaited black leather cord sits against his skin. He goes shoeless everywhere; not for him the hard leather boots the girls wear, scraping and gnarling their feet into bloody misshapenness after just a few days. Nor Boncer's steel-capped work boots; Teddy walks the prickled ground and rough floorboards always barefoot, protected by his beauty.

In the night Verla has visions of those feet crucified, a thick rusty nail driven through, piercing and splintering the fine bones, the golden skin.

The off milk smell rises up at her. She stares at the bowl, willing herself to eat. They will be out in the heat and the work shortly. DIGNITY & RESPECT IN A SAFE & SECURE ENVIRONMENT. She will soon be starving.

Beneath the faded wallpaper and the mantelpiece, Boncer— older than Teddy, peevish—stares out at the younger man through the open window, fondling his stick, fingers softly tracing the knobbled stitches of the seams. In his narrow, sulking face as he stares out at the younger man is some restless longing, or envy.

Verla forces herself back to the dish, lowering her spoon, lifting the thickened clots, holding her breath—but she can't help it: the milk revolts her and she drops the spoon as a convulsive retch hurtles up through her, and she knows from the instant soft sound of the girls' turning bonnets and their inhaled breath that Boncer is beside her with his stick raised.

She braces, bowing her head, but since the first day—the big girl, Barbs, with the broken jaw—he has not hit any of them above the neck. Barbs's entire face now is swollen, purple-black, and she cannot eat anything, even these soggy flakes.

To look at her now it is hard to remember the sheer physical charge she used to have, ploughing freestyle through the water. Fast lane to the Olympics, they said, till she had to open her mouth about the 'sports massages'. On the coach's hotel bed. And then the whole team called her *some slurry from Cronulla* and that was it, no Olympic Dream for Barbs. Now across the table her broad shoulders hunch, and she can barely open her mouth at all. At the first meal Boncer tossed a waxed paper straw on the table before her and hissed, *Don't lose it*. She draws it out at each meal, bent and wet, its end sodden and ragged.

Boncer is beside Verla and she can smell his body, sour as the milk. She stares at the table, waiting for the strike, but instead his dry white fingers come into her field of vision, picking up the bowl. She hears him sniff it, and can tell from the expression of Lydia across the table that he has made a face. But he only drops the bowl in front of her again and says tiredly, *Just fucken eat it*.

They are all surprised when he does not belt her but shuffles from the room, bangs out through the screen door to talk to Teddy.

The girls stare at each other. They scrape bowls and tinkle spoons, eating in silence. Then the whispering starts up, barely audible. Where is this? they rustle. Why haven't their families come? Will they be raped, tortured, starved, killed?

'Shuddup,' yells Boncer from the veranda.

The bonnets point back at their bowls, in silence. Boncer begins murmuring again to Teddy.

Then this, hissed: 'It's a reality show.'

Hetty, the cardinal's girl with the burnt arm, has spoken. Bonnets swivel. The silence stretches.

She whispers again, 'Like *The Bachelor*, but more edgy.'

Her sister works at Channel Ten. The winner gets two hundred thousand.

Hetty has a short, strong body, and inside the balloon of the bonnet her face is broad and flat. Her burnt arm rests on the table beside her bowl, wrapped in the ragged grey toilet paper Boncer gave her to wind around and around it. Verla does not want to look at the arm.

Outside, they hear Teddy. 'You can't just *decide* you have chronic fatigue syndrome, man. A doctor's gotta diagnose it.'

Boncer replies, sounding hurt, that he has all the symptoms.

Hetty whispers on: this is why they are all here, have been chosen. The scandals and all that. The bonnets listen, fixated, gaping. There will be challenges, says Hetty. Maybe even today the first elimination. She nods in awe at her own whispered words. Then the bonnets begin to nod with her, to bob and jerk around from Hetty to one another, disbelief becoming understanding. They begin mouthing inaudible questions.

Verla is visited by another fantasy: seizing Boncer's stick and unleashing herself with extravagant fury on Hetty, who has stopped talking now and sits back, smug, ferrying lumps of soft white bread from a plate to her mouth with her grubby good hand, back and forth, chewing steadily beneath the shadow of her bonnet. She meets Verla's gaze and stares back, her fleshy pink lips moving wetly, her tongue working to dislodge the sticky glutinous bread from her gums.

The Catholic cardinal, the never-published photographs of almost-underage Hetty, just sixteen and, it was said, lying like a fat happy baby in the purple satin and gold brocade. What the cardinal had seen close up, Verla knows now, was Hetty's wet red mouth, the coarse black eyebrows, potent with some ferocious carnality. He saw what Verla could see now, that Hetty was a little muscled dog that knew how to bite, and how to indiscriminately fuck. If she were a male the pink crayon of her dick would be always out.

People have thought this about Verla. She knows that; she read the comments at first. They've more or less said it to her face. But with Hetty it is true. The sour milk smell, the clotted mess of what Hetty is saying, the stink of her body all rise up in a curdled mist. Hetty is repulsive, a liar. Hetty can be blamed.

At the other end of the table Yolanda Kovacs sits, saying nothing, but watching Hetty with open, marvelling contempt. As she turns her gaze away she catches Verla's eye. Their bonnets sweep off in opposite directions. Verla will align herself with no-one.

One of the girls, on the verge of tears, begs Hetty in a plaintive whisper, 'But how—how do you *know* this?' It is scrawny Lydia from the cruise liner, left for dead in the toilets. Anonymous, unnamed, face blurred or blacked out, voice altered in every interview for her own protection. Well, now she has no protection and there beneath her bonnet is her gormless little face, small red-rimmed eyes, her prim thin-lipped mouth. And she has a name, Lydia Scicluna. She continues pleading into Hetty's face: Where are the cameras? How will the challenges be decided? Who will judge?

Verla can bear no more. She reaches over and puts her hand firmly down over the cruise girl's curled fist. 'She's making it up. It's not television. It's real.'

When Hetty's indignant mouth drops open, Verla says, 'Your arm is getting worse.' And all the girls stare then at Hetty's grotesquely puffing arm, its filthy wrapping doing little to stop the oozing pus.

'Boncer,' Verla calls out loud, staring Hetty down, hearing the girls gasp at her malice. Nobody has said his name before now. Verla has begun separating herself: she is not one of them.

Boncer is instantly back in the room, groping at his side for his stick, Teddy at his heels. Boncer comes to Verla with the stick raised. She wills herself not to flinch, looks into his face. She sees the white head of the pimple crowning at his chin. 'She needs something for her arm; it's getting infected.'

Boncer rolls his eyes at her, then glances at the burn and then away. He sneers, 'Who are you, Florence fucken Nightingale?', but there is something uneasy in his voice.

She keeps her eyes on the pimple head, white in the angry red swell. She tries not to anticipate the stick, fear jingling along her veins. Hetty's bonnet points floorwards. 'She'll get septicaemia.' To bait them, to make something happen.

Hetty's bonnet jerks up then and she stares down its barrel at Verla in sudden terror. 'What's that?' All her bravado gone.

Teddy leans in to peer across the table, down at Hetty's arm. He rears back in revulsion, crying, 'Ugh!' He reaches into his pocket and pulls out a small clear plastic bottle of hand sanitiser. Still staring at the greening pus and scum of Hetty's burn he squirts some of the gel into his left palm, pockets the bottle and rubs his smooth hands together. He tosses the bottle to Boncer, who does the same.

When they've gone the mentholated smell fills the room.

Hetty is crying now. The other girls slump in silence, some looking away, some staring at the glistening, spreading pus in the shallow pit of the burn.

Hetty confesses. She doesn't know anything, she made up the reality show. 'But what else could it *be*?' she wails through her sobs.

Nobody knows. They have been here almost a week. Nobody has come, nothing has happened but waiting and labour and dog kennels and DIGNITY & RESPECT and beatings and fear and a pile of concrete guttering, and now perhaps infection is coming too.

Verla feels Yolanda Kovacs watching her from the end of the table.

• • •

Soon they are toiling again with the concrete blocks under the hot cloudless sky. They are to move a pile of concrete guttering pieces from one side of the buildings to the other. No explanation or reason except it has to be done for *when Hardings comes*. The pile is as high as the roofline of the house; higher than the kennel roof.

The pieces must have been dumped here by tip truck or crane—each chunk of concrete weighs thirty kilos at least—but Verla has looked and looked and can find no road. There must have been one once, when this place was in use as a sheep station, or maybe a wheat farm, but any access road has long been overgrown. She can only discern the same faint flattened track over the grass, trailing into the distance in the direction they marched the first day.

When Verla understands it she nearly drops to the ground. The girls are to build a road for Hardings.

She trudges back and forth with the others, taking her turn to reach in and yank at the sharp angles of the concrete length and drag it free of the pile, careful not to set the mammoth pieces clunking and sliding, which happens every hour or so. All the girls have scrapes and cuts on their arms and hands from the concrete edges, from overbalancing into the pile or dropping a block. She drags a concrete log towards her, lugs the dead weight up against her body, hugging it to her. Sweat runs down her arms inside the rough fabric of her tunic, chafing and rasping. Her shoulders and forearms ache with the strain as she turns to walk.

Each footstep over the flat dead ground sets off a spangle of grasshoppers into the air before her. Small black flies dart at her mouth and eyes, trapping themselves beneath the bonnet visor. She reaches the other side, panting, and drops the block, stumbling backwards so as not to hit her feet. She bends over, hands on her knees, breathes noisily. It is only the first hour.

Every two hours they are allowed a ten-minute break. They flop on their backs in the orange dirt, too worn out to speak, and guzzle the minerally water Teddy carries in a plastic bucket, passing a chipped white mug from girl to girl.

Verla turns onto her side to get the sun off her face, dozes a minute. When she opens her eyes it's to the soft white face of Isobel a little way off, resting on her grimy hands, eyes closed, her mouth slack. Strange seeing that face in the flesh. Verla remembers another close-up: the Sunday-night interview, Izzy's smooth peachy face and her big glassy blue eyes filling the screen, the furrow between her soft blonde eyebrows. The airline CEO meanwhile hurrying his wife and children onto a first-class flight to Europe. Izzy's soft trembling voice speaking of her ruined career, of justice that must be done. And beyond the screen, behind it all, the voices of girls everywhere snorting into their vodkas, *not as if he even raped her*, sneering *all that for a snapped bra strap!* And imagine him going for a little fatty like that! Quite pretty in the face though, it was argued; Mile-High Izzy could maybe be a plus-sized model if she wanted. But still.

In the cell next to Verla's, Izzy has not stopped crying at night in her thin high whimper. Half the time she seems most distraught about the Chloé boots, bought with the settlement and only worn three times before she was taken. After just a few days Verla knows the sounds of Izzy's crying almost as well as her own. But *seeing* her up close is different, and so she stares now at famous pretty-but-fat television Izzy lying exhausted in the dirt, a grubby bonnet tied tight beneath her soft chin, her cheeks dotted with infected mosquito bites, oily with dust and tears, her closed eyes ringed with shadow, a yellowing crust of spit in the corner of her dry lips. All that money, Chloé boots and all, and now look at her.

Above Izzy's head, far off in the west, a low, deep purple bank of storm clouds smears the sky. Somewhere, far away, it is raining. But here the air is as dry as the hard yellow ground, and Verla tastes nothing but dust.

Boncer blows his whistle. Izzy stirs, they roll over, crawl to their knees.

'At least we should all lose some weight,' whispers Izzy to Verla, pushing herself up from the ground.

• • •

Teddy and Boncer stand with their arms folded, inspecting the work on the road, shooting the breeze while the girls toil on their knees.

Sometimes Teddy brings his breakfast with him, eating from a red plastic bowl with a spoon. He does not eat with the girls nor even with Boncer, who breakfasts somewhere away from the girls. But Teddy has his special collection of jars and plastic-lidded tubs lined up along one bench in the kitchen, each container sticky-taped with a homemade label of lined note paper: TEDDY'S FOOD DO NOT TOUCH scrawled in thick black marker.

Yolanda once unscrewed the lids and sniffed, then wrinkled her nose and told the girls Teddy didn't need to worry, all the jars smelled like BO. The tubs contain black shreds of special teas, or ugly faded-looking dried fruits and various powders and supplements: linseed and psyllium husks and goji berries, according to Izzy, and weird bits of stuff that looks like bark.

Lydia, sweating and grunting as she hauls a long piece of concrete kerbing, murmurs to Verla that Teddy definitely has some hash somewhere, she sometimes smells it late in the night, wafting from far up in the house. She has no doubt that Teddy packs cones and gets high, the lucky bastard.

'Jesus, I would kill for some weed,' whispers Maitlynd. She and Verla squat, their backs straining as they hold the concrete block and Lydia rakes the gravel beneath it.

Up the line Boncer and Teddy stop talking and watch the girls. 'Straighter,' yells Boncer. 'That's crooked.'

They begin again.

Teddy is reciting to Boncer a list of what he would *normally* eat, back home, and Boncer is pretending to know what these things are. In the back of the fridge are more of Teddy's special foods, manky little plastic-wrapped blocks of things almost nobody but Teddy recognises: a grey wad of uncooked clay stuff that turns out to be some kind of yeast, and another block of solid yellow curd that smells Indonesian or something, and which Joy diagnoses as tempeh. Joy rolls her eyes at the girls for not knowing what tempeh is.

Boncer and Teddy stroll along the line of struggling, sweating girls, talking all the time. Verla thinks of slave masters in old black-and-white movies.

Teddy has a yoghurt maker in his backpack, he tells Boncer, but it doesn't work anymore, and anyway it wouldn't work with this bloody fake milk they have to drink here. Teddy is disgusted by the paint-thick white UHT milk. He used to only drink soy, he says wistfully, scratching at the wispy goatee that has begun to crawl down his neck.

He took the yoghurt maker from the last place he lived, where his then sort-of girlfriend Hannah (who was *amazing* at giving head) made really awesome yoghurt every day. To eat with nuts; Christ, he misses nuts, almonds especially. Boncer wants to hear more about the head, but Teddy waves his hand and says this Hannah unfortunately started to get hung up on all sorts of neurotic bullshit and ended up just giving him the shits.

The sun beats down on the girls.

'Can we have a break, please?' asks Barbs—it is always brave Barbs pushing for rest stops, even after her broken jaw that first day—and Boncer looks pained at the interruption, then looks at his watch and blows his whistle. 'Five minutes,' he snaps.

The girls mostly just drop the concrete blocks and sit where they are in the dust, too tired even to go and lie on the dried grass. They sit with their heads on their arms across their knees.

Teddy talks on about this Hannah and her long ugly toes, how they didn't curl neatly in descending order like girls' toes should but stuck straight out in a horrible separated way. He said how, for a not-bad-looking chick, she was remarkably unattractive when she cried. She was also way, way too hairy. In general. Teddy likes them natural but, let's face it, some of them are, like, *really* hairy. Both Boncer and Teddy shudder in disgust, looking at the girls where they sit slumped in the dirt.

• • •

Something had gone out in that cardinal's girl, Hetty, by the time they got back. Yolanda was first in the door, to find Hetty still sat there at the table, a fresh pile of dunny paper beside her and her fugly bloated arm resting, wound upwards, on the table. But her bonnet was off, fallen on the floor. Her pale bald head gleamed in the gloom. Now and then she used the dunny paper to blot at the liquid seeping from her wound. She'd been crying all day, by the look of her, and now sat motionless, head turtle-low on her neck, barely moving as they all clomped in. Shit scared she was, right down deep inside, more scared than all the rest of them now.

The girls trooped in, staring at the poor bitch. Mostly the staring was out of pity, but Yolanda felt some other instinct shivering too, same as happened among the hens in her nana's chook yard. The button eyes taking a good look, circling, sizing up the weak. Looking around to see who might go in for a lunge, for the first darting, investigating peck.

The girls fell to the benches, most of them too tired to hold their heads up and keep on staring. Except old Verla Learmont, the cabinet minister's moll with a pole up her university arse, who gawked at Hetty but didn't look so pleased with herself as she was this morning, predicting gangrene. In fact she looked green-sick, like she thought she might have brought this down on Hetty herself. Maybe she did.

Yolanda watched Verla slide in next to the burnt girl, trying to look into her face, but Hetty didn't seem to notice, just stared at the table out of her sickly eyes. They all watched then as Verla got up and scuffed out the door and along the hallway to the kitchen, then came back with a big plastic cup of water and set it down in front of Hetty. Who just kept staring.

Behind Verla came Boncer with his stick. It seemed Verla would not be hit or even yelled at this time. He stood, annoyed, and pointed his stick at the cup. 'Drink it,' he ordered Hetty, so she pulled the cup towards her, took a little weary drink. Still in her turtleish dreaming sickness, but she sipped. All the other parched, sticky-mouthed girls would have to wait, watching Hetty drink, and Yolanda joined them in hating her for being so slow.

Then Boncer said, 'Christ al-fucking-mighty. Come on then.' He grabbed Hetty's upper arm and dragged her to her feet as she howled.

The bonnets jerked up everywhere to see this, Hetty letting out a bawl and her good hand shooting out to grab at Verla's sleeve and not letting go, so strong, no matter how Verla tried to prise her fingers off. They saw Boncer shrugging and saying, 'You too then, looks like,' clipping Verla's lead to Hetty's and violently yanking so the two of them stumbled away from the table and out of the door.

Fat Izzy from the airline reached out and snatched up Hetty's cup and drank down all the water in it before the next girl could knock the cup from her hands. It bounced, empty, to the floor.

They heard Boncer shouting in the corridor, 'March.'

• • •

Hetty marches with her left arm swinging, holding her bad one gingerly at her side. She doesn't ask where they are going, and nor does Verla. They follow Boncer through dark cardboard corridors, through the gloom of rooms leading into other rooms, more passageways, closed verandas, into and out of dark, narrow spaces, light green ones. The house is a concertina opening and lengthening and fanning out before them, compressing and closing behind. In the dusty weatherboard rooms as they pass through are signs of former lives: chests of drawers half open, framed faded watercolours flyspecked and hanging crookedly. A folded dusty swag on the floor of one room, a bare mattress on a black iron bed in another. In one dark corridor Boncer suddenly leans sideways and pulls a door closed, but not before Verla sees it must be *his*: sees a red sports bag unzipped, spilling clothes, a threadbare pink bath towel draped from a cupboard door. The corner of a pale blue bedsheet hanging to the floor, a balled pair of dirty sports socks. The vision disappears behind the white door with a dented brass handle. Boncer jerks around to inspect Hetty and Verla, to see what they have seen. They keep their eyes to the floor.

'I said *march*.'

Verla swings her arms, blinking hard to seal the image in. *Remember where we are*, retracing in memory the corridors, the spindly French doors leading from one room to another, the turns they have taken left and right, the steps up and down. She is quickly lost. All that remains in her mind are columns of light pressing through tall green curtains, the pink towel, doorways opening on to other doors.

Now they are outside again, clomping along another rickety veranda, down three steps and around a rusted water tank on a rotting wooden platform, up another set of steps, and now stopped before yet another door on another veranda. Hetty is breathing hard, swallowing. Boncer lightly kicks the door ajar but doesn't go in.

'Something for you, Nancy,' he calls out, looking up at the veranda roof and fingering his pimple. So it is true: Nancy. A woman.

There is a muffled yelp from behind the door. Hetty and Verla wait, not daring to look anywhere but up, following Boncer's gaze. All three stand in the stifling heat, watching the honeycombed grey nugget of a wasps' nest forming on the tip of a rusted nail spiking from a beam above them. Three slow, long-bodied wasps weave their way, swaying, to the nest, finally landing, wriggling, disappearing into its holes.

At last Boncer shakes his head and mutters *fuck's sake* beneath his breath. He shouts, 'They're coming in,' and shoves the chained girls through the door with the hard bulge of his stick.

They stumble in, Hetty hissing in pain. The room is large, flooded with light. There are waist-high metal trolleys, and a leather-padded thigh-high table that could be a bed. It has a short blue plastic sheet with stippled white paper towelling over it, and a flat, mouldy-looking pillow. From the end of the bed extend two wooden prongs, each attached to a small, sturdy brown leather stirrup belt, unbuckled. On the floor between the prongs is a steel bucket.

They can see nobody in the room. Near the window is a spearmint-green metal stool with a large metal seat like a bicycle saddle. Nearby, a white plastic commode chair. A battered aluminium tray lies on a trolley beneath the window's soft spreading light, holding pieces of liver-coloured rubber tubing, metal cones and long, sharp steel instruments.

Verla's and Hetty's hands clutch at one another just as an irritated mutter comes from behind the open door. 'I'm not ready!'

The door swings shut and they are enclosed in the room with a small figure crouched on the floor, rummaging in a pile of plastic shopping bags. They stare. The elbow wings are working now at some arrangement of her clothes, her short denim skirt rucking up her pale, skinny thighs. The figure jiggles a little, squatting on her flat feet in grubby white tennis shoes.

At last she straightens, and a slight figure, a girl, stands facing them with a surprised, open-mouthed smile on her flushed face. A small round face, two dull blonde plaits just reaching her shoulders. She can be only a year or two older than Verla, perhaps twenty-three. She's shorter than Verla, though, and wears a workman's shirt far too big for her—it is made of the same thick blue cotton as Boncer's and Teddy's boiler suits. It comes nearly to the hem of her miniskirt. Two tiny gold crosses dangle from her earlobes. But what Hetty and Verla are staring at is what this Nancy has pinned to herself: bits of a child's nurse's costume. A little white apron with a thick red cross is safety-pinned crookedly across the front of her shirt. This is what she was rummaging among the bags for: the indigo velveteen cape she's now tying around her neck so it sticks out behind her, just covering her shoulders. Most monstrous of all, a little white starched origami cap with a blue stripe across it, balancing on her crown.

She watches Hetty and Verla registering all this, and grins. 'Isn't it a scream?'

They glance at each other in disbelief. Verla sees a plastic stethoscope peeking from the shirt pocket. They are truly in a madhouse.

Hetty falls against Verla, giving up, cradling her weeping arm and howling.

The girl, this Nancy, is annoyed. '*Joke*, Joyce. Jesus.'

She wipes her hands down her thighs and steps out from her nest of plastic bags to inspect the two girls. She nods at Hetty's arm, grabs it roughly. 'So what've you done to yourself, you silly bitch?'

Hetty bawls more at this injustice, yanks her arm away.

'You're not a nurse,' says Verla. She hears the low angry croak of her own voice. She sounds like an old, old woman.

Nancy steps closer, grabs Hetty's wrist again with her small strong hand and peers down at the burn. 'Pee-ew!' She rears back. 'That is *rank*.'

Verla scans the room. 'She needs antiseptic and bandages. Her arm's infected. I'll do it.'

All Nancy's girlishness vanishes in the long appraising stare she runs over Verla's body now. She stares at Verla's dirty tunic, the ridiculous bonnet. Verla feels herself inside them, reduced.

'Is that right, Miss *Verla Learmont*?' Her voice is coldly adult now, saying Verla's name—how does she know it?—with amused, disgusted pity. Junior school days come to Verla; the hot shameful moment of learning that other girls knew things you did not. That you were ugly, contemptible.

Nancy stares at her and says, 'You know what you look like? A *seahorse!*' She cackles. 'You really do.' And she does an impression, a trembling stare from bulging eyes, makes her face long, translucent, horsey. Flutters her fingers in a rapid, nervy tremor at her thighs. Verla knows it is true, she does look this way. Mad and pale and terrified.

Nancy grins, then turns to Hetty and snaps, 'Get up there,' pointing to the padded bed. Hetty will not let go her grip on Verla's arm, but Verla is suddenly sick of everything. No longer afraid, just gut weary of it all, the fear and stupidity and madness of this sick incomprehensible game. She digs her fingers beneath Hetty's and peels her away, shoves her off, moaning, towards the bed.

Nancy clinks away in a corner with an enamel kidney dish and pungent antiseptic and turns to where Hetty now lies, her filthy arm in its rags of paper. She roars as Nancy paws off the toilet paper and begins sloshing disinfectant into the wound.

Verla turns and stands looking out of the speckled window, out through a gap in the buildings, across the dry knobbled land. She no longer cares about Hetty, about Lydia Scicluna, or Isobel Askell or little Joy or Barbs or Yolanda Kovacs. She cares nothing for any of them, for she alone will get out of here. If she is not sent for she will escape. The force of her will for this—a great charge of it thrusting up through her body—fills her. She will walk to the fence, burrow into the ground like an animal, tunnel her way free. Or find some other way, over or under or through, but she will be free.

She puts her head to the warm glass and silently draws air from the narrow gap between the sash and frame, drinking it into her lungs.

'Oh no, you don't,' snickers Nancy into her ear, and there comes a hard little snap as she closes a child's plastic handcuff painfully around Verla's wrist, snapping the other end to the radiator bar. Then she goes back to hurting Hetty on the bed.

THE GIRLS lay in their boxes staring up at the cobwebby roof beams, calling to each other, rearranging their lists of most missed things. For Rhiannon, today, it was Salada biscuits with soft butter and Vegemite. 'Oh *yeah*,' shouted Maitlynd. Then: 'No, not Saladas. *Vita*-Weats!' But the same creamy butter worming through the fantasy biscuit holes, the same stacked brick of sharp-cornered crackers in your hand as you wandered freely through your own house, eating as much as, and whenever, you wanted.

They lay there, tasting biscuits, conjuring luxuries.

Bare feet without blisters. On *carpet*. Hot showers. Vodka. Coffee. Cigarettes (the ones who never smoked were lucky; every one of the rest had fleetingly, shamefully, thought of offering herself to Teddy or Boncer for a single drag, that hot draught in the lungs, that brief and wondrous extinguishment of need).

'What about this!' From Lydia: the Pavilion at Maroubra on a hot day, watching the surfers moving across that rich greeny ocean, a Skinny Dip in your hand, and a huge plate of *fish and chips*.

They groaned. Hot chips.

'And a hot guy!' yelled Barbs.

They murmured again, out of politeness, but it was the chips that stayed in the mind.

BONCER LEANED sideways, unclipped a key from the bunch at his waist and threw it on the table before Yolanda. 'Go get more food.'

She looked at him, key in her palm. The other girls stared too. This had never happened, a key.

'Christ on a bike, you're a dumb dog. *Storeroom.*'

Five minutes or she'd cop it from his stick, he said. Adding, 'The real one,' grinning and thrusting his crotch at her as she pushed past him.

She was at the door by the time he shouted, 'March!' and as an afterthought sent the stick spinning to crash into the doorframe just beside her head. It clattered to the floor and she heard Boncer's titter floating after her as she marched, arms swinging high, the little key sharp in her fist.

It was dusk as she stepped outside, bird calls falling in light musical sweeps in the hazy air. This was the first time since arriving here that she had been allowed to walk anywhere alone, unleashed. For a moment she thought of bolting. But where would she go?

Far off, over by the ridge, a wedge-tailed eagle was pursued by ravens, wheeling and diving against the pink sky.

Five minutes. She hurried across the gravel to the faded salmon-coloured fibro shed on its crooked stumps, up the grey brick stairs, and worked the key into the padlock. The ancient trace of an ivy skeleton laced over one corner of the shed. She worked the bolt free and pushed open the door, its handle loose as a broken bone in her hand.

She'd never been in here, none of them had; they'd only seen Boncer and Nancy coming and going over the weeks, stepping down from the doorway with boxes and cartons of packaged foods, always locking the door behind them.

Inside was the stillness and disorder of abandonment. Light fell into the room through a tall, curtainless window at one end of the single room. The floorboards were thick with dust, and everywhere were towers and stacks of cardboard boxes. Some had been ripped open and the contents pillaged. There seemed no method or order to this; more as if animals had been. Yolanda thought of stories about old people dying in housing commission flats, of dogs tearing open their chests. She heard the wet rhythmic noise of animal tongues and breath, the steady, jerking tug of teeth working through muscle and organ, the crack of bone.

In the churchy quiet she felt herself suddenly flood with fatigue. She would like to lie down in here, build a small house of cardboard boxes, tear up cereal packets and pour out the contents. Make a nest for herself from no-brand cornflakes and bran sticks and faded popped rice.

Boncer would be waiting with his stick. Yolanda fought the madness off, must *gather information*. This she had planned in the first days, when adrenaline still filled her waking hours. *Escape* was the word she'd thought over and over back then, only weeks ago, but now that word seemed stupid, as childish as pixies or talking teddy bears.

She looked, counted, committed to memory, working her way through the columns of boxes, left to right along the windowless wall. Thirty-four boxes, each containing twenty-seven Black and Gold two-minute noodle packs. Nineteen cartons of baked beans, thirty-six cans in each. Twenty-four boxes of Homebrand rice bubbles, twelve of bran flakes. Eighteen five-kilo tins of powdered milk. Even Boncer and Nancy and Teddy now ate this shit, when at the start they'd had real food, stored and cooked somewhere else. You could smell it at night. Onions, meat. The girls lay in their kennels in the heat, mouths filling with saliva.

She went on counting. Twenty-six boxes of macaroni cheese, and there, glowing, a single carton of *cake mix*. She ripped it open, pulled out one of the boxes—Lemon Butter Cake—tore it open and thrust the blank foil sachet down into her underpants. She would eat it in bed.

• • •

Later, she stood side by side with Verla at the scullery sink, Verla lifting the chipped bowls out of the tepid grey dishwashing water for Yolanda to dry. What had she seen in the storeroom? murmured Verla.

'Nothing,' Yolanda said. 'Noodles.'

'How many?'

She could feel Verla looking at her. 'Dunno,' she said. *Thirty-four, twenty-seven, nineteen, thirty-six.* She knew Verla knew. She said, 'Didn't have time to count, he'd already tried to hit me once.'

Verla said nothing.

They stood, dipping the smeared dishes in the water, picking off the dried yellow paste with their dirty fingernails. Yolanda had a sudden urge to tell Verla the truth.

'I wasn't tricked, you know,' Yolanda said.

'What?' said Verla.

'Into coming here. The rest of you all said that when you got taken, you were tricked. I wasn't tricked; I fought. I knew those arseholes wanted me gone.'

So Yolanda told her story to Verla, standing there with her hands in dishwater. Told of the late-night meeting, how Darren and Robbie drove her there, waited outside the room. Let her go in by herself, and there were the CEO and human resources and the *gender adviser*, and there was the money offered, written right there on paper.

Yolanda looked at the dirty water circling Verla's motionless wrists and told how she knew it was lies coming out of that gender chick's mouth, else why was this happening at night, why was the gender chick in trackie daks and no make-up instead of jackets and heels for the cameras? All lies talked at Yolanda, this bitch nodding about community standards and *completely unacceptable* but all twitchy, very nervy, and the men nervous as hell too, standing by staring down at the table with their thick arms crossed over their chests, wearing weekend clothes, T-shirts and cargo pants, not the handsome suits with bulging blue ties they wore on television getting into and out of cars with cameras all around. And over and again they said it, *unacceptable* and *inappropriate*, and Yolanda spat, 'What, like being late to the fucken opera? Like what happened to me was a case of bad *manners*?' And she kept looking at the door thinking where's Darren, where's Robbie, but the gender chick kept on and on with legal shit and recompense and gestures of goodwill and all like that and the two dudes looked on, nodding at the table all solemn, giving Yolanda their sad little *there's-a-good-girl* smiles.

Verla and Yolanda could hear clicks and frogs outside because it was getting dark, and Yolanda gripped a shiny wet plate to her chest with crossed hands as she told Verla how even at that point her mind didn't actually know, her dumb dog's mind was trying to believe this shit—but oh, her body knew. Like always, her dumb dog's *body* knew, and when she looked at that crescent of polished fingernail beside the space on the paper and the pen just there and a little *x* marks the spot, it was what her body knew that refused to take it *this* time, that pushed her up out of that chair towards the door, and then the large hands came gripping and it was her body kicking like fuck and spitting and screaming as the gender chick walked into the corner of the room and put her face in *her* hands, and Yolanda bucked and shrieked. And outside that room Robbie and her darling Darren knew what was happening, and had delivered her up.

'So. I wasn't tricked. And I *fought*.'

• • •

Verla knows Yolanda is telling the truth. And then, with the image of the kicking, bucking Yolanda who understood something terrible was coming, Verla knows that a month has gone by and she will not be released. She understands, like a bucket of cold water coming down, that nobody is looking for her. There are no petitions, no Facebook protest groups, no legal challenges, no private negotiations. The memory of the agreement she signed—oh, her own stupidity—makes Verla's face hot. Georgie Mullan, chief of staff, has made that thing never exist, has burned the Walt Whitman too, and somewhere Andrew is nodding sadly at Georgie's *all for the best*, believing her bullshit about Verla leaving the country, Verla in hiding, Verla under protection, that stone-hearted Georgie steering Andrew back to his wife and children and everything is for the best.

And Verla the Stupid let this happen, eating oysters and handing over the Whitman 'for safekeeping', gratefully signing fake legal papers, at the same moment as Yolanda roared and kicked and bit. Yolanda resisted, but Verla complied. *She is stronger than me.*

The other girls have muttered to one another all through the days, forming pacts, whining, coaxing, telling their stories, inspecting each other for ticks, for nits. Comforting, telling lies, making alliances. Crying for their mothers and fathers, for home, and Verla has felt shame and pity for them, knowing Andrew would get her back, believing herself protected and missed.

She wishes for one thing only now, here at the sink: to be back in that quiet restaurant so she could send her wineglass shattering and snatch up that fancy French steak knife and push it deep and downwards into Georgie Mullan's throat.

Yolanda has told the truth about being taken, but is lying about the storeroom: she has seen things in there she's not telling, things she won't reveal. Yolanda and Verla hold themselves apart, for survival. This is their bond.

Verla knows this because she too has her private mind, containing things she will not tell: her dreams, and the horse. She has heard her white horse in the night. The others have heard it too, but they think it's a dingo, a possum, they think it is Boncer or Teddy or Nancy even, scuffing about outside the kennels, wandering in the dark. Only Verla has seen its white flank, passing close to her window in the moonlight, and she has smelled its breath. It lifted its long, fine head, held still in the dark, looking at Verla, breathing quiet and deep as she looked back at it, breathing her own quiet and deep reply.

Come for me, she has whispered to it, and the horse knows. It will come.

In the days, lifting concrete, she secretly scans the hills. This morning she saw its handkerchief-flash, just for an instant, up on the far ridge, in the black scrubby bush. One night it will come, she will crawl out, somehow, and climb onto that horse's broad white back and lie down over its long body, twine her fingers in its mane, and it will take her away.

Sink water sploshes. Yolanda takes another dish from Verla's hands.

Boncer comes in, chewing something. He pulls a chair up and sits, leaning back, legs wide, watching Yolanda work. Watching Yolanda's body, Verla knows. Another thing she will not tell.

Verla sees herself whirl from the sink, hurl a spinning plate to strike Boncer in the head. Sees her own strong calloused hands wrenching that chair apart, taking the splintered end of its broken leg to stab Boncer into pulp, her knees on his chest, her shoulders working the pole of the broken leg hard and fast, mashing and grinding, Boncer's face unrecognisable, his blood soaking into the pits of the ancient linoleum.

She hands another dish, dripping, to Yolanda. Outside, the cockatoos are starting up for the evening. Boncer sits, staring at Yolanda, running the leash slowly through his hands.

When they finish the dishes he clips them together and leads them back out to the cells. It is not yet dark enough to see the stars, but the girls look up for them nonetheless.

THE MANY faults of Hannah are Teddy's favourite topic, and he returns to it often with Boncer. It is as though this is what he meditates on, breathing in a tantric way through his long, demanding yoga sessions on the veranda. On hot days he rolls his boiler suit down, right down to his hips, and the sweat gleams on his beautiful bare back as he rolls through his poses. Teddy has sharp pink nipples and his chest is covered with light golden hairs.

Down at the roadwork, Rhiannon and Leandra agree that they wouldn't mind doing it with Teddy. At first there is a general consensus that Teddy would be all right in the sack, but the more they hear him complain about this Hannah of the past, the more it seems that sex with Teddy would be like sharing a bed with someone having sex with himself. Hannah and her hairy legs, the thick way she breathed that he didn't like, the way she fucking *nagged* him about pointless, bourgeois shit, and also her politics, which were pretty immature—all of these faults of Hannah are things the girls can imagine in themselves, and they begin to feel small and exposed, and it becomes more difficult to imagine wanting sex under Teddy's intricately critical gaze. Teddy is the kind of guy, Izzy eventually declares, that would be out telling his mates how small your tits are the minute after you've sucked his dick. It is true, the girls agree, and after that they despise Teddy almost as much as Boncer.

• • •

At night Boncer and Teddy still come to sit and smoke in the rotting cane chairs. Verla hears them talking about Boncer's Scampr profile. He wonders about the responses lining up for him, worries what he's missed, the momentary blossoming of love hearts and lipstick kisses of all the women ready and waiting, wanting him, but who for lack of a reply now may have moved on.

'. . . *the way a woman should be treated, so if you wanna dance the night away*—I put that at the end,' Boncer recites, wistful.

There's a silence before Teddy says, 'Sounds great, man.'

'You weren't even listening, you prick.'

'I was,' protests Teddy. 'I was just thinking.'

There comes the woolly flare of a struck match. They have not yet run out of tobacco but are rationing. Teddy's weed ran out several days ago. From her bed Verla imagines their two stupid faces illuminated for a moment, hears the suck and exhalation and smells the richness of the smoke, sees Teddy with one bare foot hooked across his knee, Boncer's skinny legs straight out, stretched back in the sinking chair.

'Chicks dig dancing,' Teddy says in his smoke-husked voice. 'You could practise with Nancy.'

Boncer sighs—'Nah'—but there is longing in his voice.

Verla's pulse knows what's coming. A red-bellied black snake moves through her mind, sliding through the grass.

'So . . .' says Boncer slyly. 'Which one would you?' Then he and Teddy both at once say, *Kovacs*, and break into sniggers.

Teddy starts his usual warning about shitting in your own nest but trails off into silence. It is a long time since they have mentioned the bonuses.

A hopeful tension enters Teddy's voice then, when he says, 'So you reckon Hardings are coming, this time?'

Another pause. Moths tick against the tin.

'First week of next month, they reckon,' says Boncer. 'But they've said that every time.'

A glum silence falls. The night swells, and Verla's snake slithers back into hibernation beneath the floor. She sees Teddy gloomily stroking the long arch of his foot resting across his knee.

'Cunts,' says Boncer.

After they have gone, Verla stands for a time at the window looking up at the stars. Eventually she goes to the bed and falls in and out of sleep, straining to hear the soft, irregular steps and chewing breath of her moonlight horse, but it does not come.

part two:
AUTUMN

CLOUDS COLLECT and steepen, build then collapse, silver empires rising and falling in the vast blue skies.

Months have passed.

They no longer ask about going home, no longer strain to listen for aircraft or truck or tractor sounds. The bonnets are worn soft, the shoe leather too. Their days are a rhythm of marching, labour, sleep, a little food from the packets in the storeroom. Some of the girls have sickened and mended, others still limp. Barbs's broken jaw has healed, though badly; she will never bite straight. Hetty's burnt arm is angry with a stretched, glossy scar of deep red, but the itching has almost stopped.

Boncer still carries his stick everywhere and occasionally savagely strikes, but it mostly hangs unused from his belt. He no longer has the daily energy for it. Teddy ties up his dreadlocks now with rags torn from Hardings tea towels; DIGNIT and PECT and ONMENT, reads the tiny blue print on torn white linen rags winding through his murky fronds. Nancy has abandoned her miniskirt in favour of an oversized boiler suit like the men's, which she wears with sleeves and trouser legs rolled. Her costume props have gone except for the toy nurse's cap, which she still wears bobby-pinned to her ratty blonde hair. The cap is bent and grimy with finger marks, but she won't give it up. She complains all the time of boredom, until Boncer shouts at her, *For fuck's sake you're worse than them*, and then she sits sulking on the veranda, eyes rimmed red, watching Boncer, trying to please him.

The girls are still clipped together when taken to and from the cells. In the field they labour, chipping weeds, shovelling gravel, raking. The pile of concrete chunks has gone, the pieces laid out end to end into the distance. The road corridor has been cleared, the hard dry dirt graded with their hands and ancient hoes and rakes. Edges have been dug and sloped to stop erosion. As they scraped and cleared the knee-high grass they have shrieked and dropped their tools and leaped from the slithering path of brown snakes and red-bellied blacks, or the stomping shuffle of the thick-necked, weaving goannas. Bird calls drop from the skies all day long and, taught by Leandra, the bird nerd from the army, they recognise them now: not just the screams of cockatoos and corellas or the squawking lorikeets, but also the floatier melodies of wagtails, butcherbirds, thrushes and kites. At night the mournful, mournful stone curlews cry.

Hardings is still coming, they say. They believe Hardings is coming.

The girls' bodies have hardened, thickened with muscle. Their skin has grown tougher under manual work and sunburn and dirt. Most of them have lost their bonnets, and they scratch furiously at their thick, ragged new hair. Somebody always now has lice.

The sun is losing its heat, and the nights are growing longer. The darkness creeps in early, and stays.

A GREAT huntsman spider patrols Verla's ceiling, lurking in the same spot for days at a time. The dogboxes are cooler now in the nights. Verla dreams of clawing at faces, spitting and fighting.

One morning she wakes in stillness. Boncer has not come bashing on the tin walls, but she can tell by the quality of the light that it is no longer early morning, and she can hear the others shifting on their beds.

'What's happening?' she calls out.

Nothing, they say. From Verla's window she can see no movement up at the house, there is no sound. Nobody knows anything.

Then Hetty yells cheerfully, 'A sleep-in!' and begins reporting last night's dream. As usual, it is of food. But it is not the food she knows. She dreamed she was on safari, that she was

THE NATURAL WAY OF THINGS

a sleek animal, a *predator*. She dreamed of pushing her sharp teeth through the soft belly flesh of a zebra. She describes an ecstatic moment of puncture. Of burying her face in blood and still-pulsing wet flesh.

'That's not about food, it's about sex!' yells Maitlynd from three cells away.

'*So* gross.' That is Lydia, from down near the end.

'Lesbian sex!' yells Maitlynd.

'You *wish*,' Hetty sneers in reply.

They settle into quiet again, sinking back into the creaking beds. The cicadas start up outside and Verla falls into a loose, shimmery sleep.

When she wakes there is still no sound but the buzz of flies and the ticking of the roof and the walls as the sun gets higher.

At last, Leandra calls through the walls, 'Joy, sing for us?'

Joy has barely opened her mouth since she arrived, and has told almost nothing about what happened on *PerforMAXX*. All they really know is what everyone knows from the papers and the court case, of Gordo's fatherly 'bear hugs', the weigh-ins and threats, the on-screen faltering and tears everyone thought were about the competition, about Joy losing her nerve and wasting her talent, when it was really about what Gordo liked to do to her in the soundproofed cave of the studio when the others had all gone home. And Joy got eliminated and stopped singing for good.

There is silence from her cell.

'Please?' says Rhiannon, but no answer comes. They know she won't; she never has, no matter how many times they have asked. Hetty has started up again about her dream, when a low rhythmic scratching sound is heard. It is a sound both familiar and strange, and it's coming from Leandra's cell. Hetty stops talking, they all strain to hear as the scratching grows louder, knowing yet not quite placing this sound, wanting it to go on. *Chunk*-a *chunk*-a *chunk*-a, comes the scratching, something they recognise from long ago. And then it works: the scratching calls up Joy's voice, compelled by rhythm alone, her body responding. The beat coaxes it from her, strong and rich and clear. Verla hears it, they all hear it, travelling along the beams of the roof and the ripples of the tin. That voice, lush and low, and it's the first lines of *Rolling in the Deep*, Joy's song, the one she was going to win with. The cover song every teenager in the country watched her take possession of each week, practising at the piano, crying in corners, starting again, getting better, her voice growing in power and conviction. The girls lie completely still, listening to the dark honeyed voice of Joy, growing louder. Then the second verse begins and a drumbeat rises up from the boards beneath Lydia's heavy boot, and then Rhiannon joins her, a hollow tribal booming from the tin wall of her cell. Then Maitlynd starts drumming too, and then Barbs, and this deep jungle beat seems to rise up from the earth itself, spreading through the fibres of the floors and walls, through their bodies, along the cells from girl to girl, and above it Joy's voice climbs, and soon the whole kennel building is thumping with this belly-driven rhythmic song. Joy's voice strengthens and soars, crying out with bitter fury, crying out the scars on her captive heart, singing up from the depths of her despair. The girls are all standing now, beating at the drums of their walls, beating out with boots and fists the months of grief and rage, each drumming for herself but most of all for Joy, until at last the song is ending and cell by cell the drumbeat eases and quietens and stops, until the only sound is Joy's pure human voice: steady, rich and bitter. The voice of Joy, who almost had it all.

• • •

It is mid-afternoon by the time Nancy's skittering footsteps come down the gravel track. They hear her enter the dark corridor, sniffing liquidly as she moves along the line of dogbox doors and calls, 'Get up, you lazy slags.' But she's taking longer than Boncer does, struggling to turn the keys in the rusting padlocks.

Barbs shouts, 'What's going on, Nancy? Why have we not been let out?'

Verla lies, listening.

'Mind your beeswax,' Nancy says, but she sounds nervous.

Out in the daylight they stand. They are still bristling with the power of Joy's bitter broken-hearted song, and even though Nancy could not have missed the noise she behaves as if she heard nothing. Verla looks along the line, sees with new eyes how changed they all are. How dirty and aged and toughened. Would they be recognisable now to their own mothers? Their hair returning as thick pelts over their heads, like possum fur. Heavy with dirt, oily as feathers, thinned and coarsened by the dry rubbish they eat. Verla's is the worst, they tell her. Bushy and dull, like coarse fur beneath her fingers. She wouldn't have a clue what she looks like. In this whole place there is no mirror, except for the shard Izzy was once found with, out in the paddock one day. She had found it, rust-speckled, among the spider webs and rat droppings behind one of the troughs outside the old laundry and carried it gingerly inside her tunic. Then slunk from the roadwork at midday, off into a paddock, standing there holding it high in her two hands, flicking and tilting it, scanning the sky. There had to be satellites up there—Google Earth, hello?—and *someone* would see a mirror flash. Rhiannon snorted that Google Earth didn't bother updating shithole landscapes in the middle of the desert where nobody lived, and though they all knew Rhiannon must be right, Izzy was hell-bent on rescue and stood out there with her mirror even after they yelled at her that Boncer was coming. He beat her so badly she still couldn't walk properly, and that was well over a month ago.

'Where is Boncer?' Yolanda asks Nancy now.

They all eye her as she moves along clipping them together. They could easily overpower her, Verla thinks—Nancy is skinnier than any of them, pasty-skinned, ratty-haired. But what would be the point? Where would they go? The strength of Joy's song is leaching away from her, the romance of it turning foolish now out in the hard light of the day. The thickening bush creeps down the ridge, the nights are getting cold.

Nancy clips them together, one then another. At Boncer's name she blinks rapidly down at her busy fingers. Something is happening.

'He's . . . in a meeting!' she says, grimacing, trying to extract a key from the sticky lock of Joy's leash.

The girls snort, looking at each other. Verla swats at a mosquito. The large, slow insects have been getting worse, breeding down in the muddy shallows of the dam. All the girls are covered in bites, some of them red and scabby with infection.

'What fucking meeting!' It is Lydia, her little black eyes glittering sarcasm, hands on her hips. For a second Verla sees her on the cruise ship dance floor, chin tilted, glossy hair up, the black sequinned boob tube that was in all the photos. Those eyelashes thick with lust and mascara, wide sexy mouth all teeth and laughing. Before everything that happened, when Lydia was just a pretty Maltese girl at a party, a little drunk and up for it, when even that drug-fucked lowlife in the muscle T-shirt might have called her Lydia instead of *that thing, that black ugly dog.*

Nancy turns and slaps Lydia's face, striking hard with her flat palm. Lydia shrieks; the others cry out in shock, then grab Lydia's arm to stop her punching Nancy back.

'Mosquito, sweetie, sorry!' sings Nancy nastily. She turns back to her job, tugging hard on the leashes. 'Okay, march! You fat things.'

In the line as they tramp up the track Verla watches Barbs's thick muscled shoulders moving beneath her tunic, the strong cords of her neck, her angular skull. The unbalanced swell at the side of her face from the broken jaw. Long before today they have mastered the rhythm of marching when chained so none of them is jerked or stumbles. This way of moving, shackled together, has become part of them, unremarked, unconscious. But today they shift and step out of time, unsettled. Where is Boncer?

Verla scans the surroundings as they walk, this strangeness of Nancy leading them making her see things as new again: the leaning fences of the stock yards, the collapsed shearing shed, the low concrete corridor of the sheep dip, and the ramps and chutes to the rotting dark interior of the shed. She searches the ridge for the white horse, but she has not seen it for weeks.

She's yanked forwards. In front of her the tongue of a tattooed butterfly wing creeps from beneath the coarse fabric of Barbs's tunic—a tip of pink and orange wing, one coal-grey antenna—curling up the back of her broad red neck from her left shoulder. The line moves awkwardly as Nancy jerks on the leashes, making them trip and stumble. Verla must watch the movement of Barbs's boot heels, scuffed almost white and salty with tidemarks of sweat. Her solid calves sprout thick black hairs.

In the first month, early on, they all scratched through their tunics as their pubes grew bristling back, pulled up their skirts to ram a hand into their pants. Girls stood straddling the concrete blocks, raking like mad at their crotches, some more horrified than others at this sprouting hair, all over. Joy cried; she had never even seen her own fully grown pubes, her mother took her for waxing as soon as they began to appear. Hairless and smooth as marble was Joy, until now.

Verla no longer cares about hair, nor does Yolanda, nor Maitlynd or Hetty. But Lydia and Joy have wheedled a pair of tweezers from Nancy and spend evenings poring over each other's limbs, pincering out hairs one by one, wincing and yelping. Good for them, says Yolanda, they will be first in line when Boncer and Teddy finally decide they can have their pick.

Now and then Verla remembers with a shock that they are not children, not actually girls, but adult women, in the world, in Australia. Somewhere in this same country there are cities and the internet and governments and families and shopping centres and universities and airports and offices, all going about their business, all operating normally. Verla feels a pain rising all the way up from her lower gut at *governments*. Was Andrew still striding the corridors, giving doorstops on the steps? Giving that charged ironic gaze as he took your hand and pressed the folder into it? She gets a cold feeling now, marching, the shame of wanting his hands again, the desire in her provoked by these images of him.

The third time they met, he slid *Leaves of Grass* into her hands as he dropped her off in the city and his cab flew away. She read and read those unfathomable lines, not understanding but absorbing, so even now they drape about her memory in decorated prayers and incantations. *Rock me in billowy drowse, Dash me with amorous wet.*

The few remaining bonnets bob in the line behind Nancy. The girls have mostly abandoned the hats now, one way or another. Verla burned hers in the incinerator, and one by one the others, too, got rid of theirs when they could: tearing them into pieces and saying the mangle did it, or burying it and lying—to the point of a beating, with Yolanda—that it must have blown off the brick pile as they worked, far into the scrub. But Hetty, Maitlynd, Joy, some of the others, have grown somehow attached to theirs, and wear them always. They depend on the snug containment of their heads, covering their ears, the obscured vision. Verla can understand it, though only from a distance. She used to hold them in contempt for keeping the bonnets; not anymore. But still, for herself that limp, stinking thing felt more like a prison than this whole place.

Something is happening up the line.

Nancy has jolted them to a stop and unclips Yolanda, sends her to the storeroom for *whatever you can find*. Yolanda and Verla meet each other's eyes before she sets off.

The rest plod up the hill, up the dry wooden steps and across the hollow veranda boards. No Boncer, no Teddy. They clomp into the damp linoleum coolness of the ref, are unclipped, sit down and wait, elbows on the table, staring at their dirty fingernails. A large lone mosquito drifts across the air before Verla. She blows at it; it tumbles in the air, then recovers. It should be too cold for mosquitoes.

She returns to her fantasies in which she kills Boncer: with a heavy stone to the head, by strangulation with a leash, with a kitchen knife through the chest (they are all too blunt, she's looked). By pushing him down some stairs, from a rock, off a cliff. The most practical would be the electric fence; they could rush him and hold him there—but how to stop the shock passing through and killing them all? By snake or spider bite; she looks out for them, tries to catch them but fails. With an axe. Suffocation in his sleep. Beating in his skull with his own stick. Staking him to the ground and hoping for vultures. Before now Verla never knew she could carry such violence in her. Even when Andrew was forced to dismiss and deny her, she did not yearn for vengeance like this. Her visions are not simply of Boncer's death, nor her own freedom. The moments she dwells on are those of degradation, of Boncer abject and grovelling.

The mosquito returns, hovering, strangely large. Verla sighs, claps again at the insect. But it only sails ahead of her hands, purposeful, gliding, steady. It is too cold for mosquitoes, but this one is fat, it knows the air.

She is feeling odd. She smells peculiar too, she discovered last night when she went outside to piss in the grass, her head dropping to her chest with tiredness as she squatted. An odd smell came up from her chest. She sniffed inside her under-blouse to smell not just the familiar stink of her body, not just dirt, but something sour and sickly. She can smell it now, hovering just beyond herself. She lays her head down on the table, resting on her crossed arms.

At the whine of the mosquito in her ear she jerks upright, clapping her hands near her head. When she opens her hands it lies there, a huge squashed black thing, and her palms are bloody. Whose blood? She looks around at her sisters: their sallow, mosquito-bitten faces, the dark eyes deep in their yellowing skin, staring at the table or a wall.

They have not eaten any fresh food since they arrived here. No wonder they look so grey and sick. Verla wipes her bloody hands down the dirty pleats of her skirt, tips back in her chair. She sees then that the mottled fly-spotted ceiling is covered with the fine hairs of settled mosquitoes. Hundreds of them; not moving, not searching, not hungry. Waiting.

• • •

What fucking bollocks Nancy talked. Once Yolanda reached the cracked concrete step of the storeroom she turned around to watch the others straggling up the steps into the ref, Nancy behind them, nervily pulling at one of her own mangy plaits, searching the long veranda for signs of Boncer or Teddy.

Meeting. Who with, and how? Unless there was a phone or laptop they didn't know about. But Nancy had the wind up her, and there was a whiff of something bad coming. Something worse than usual.

The storeroom smelled of dust and cardboard, and in one glance Yolanda discovered what she had already known to be true: by winter the food would be running out.

Yolanda had kept count over the months, and now she found she had been almost right. The light coming in the spotty window revealed a room full of large empty boxes. She shuffled through them in the dry, echoing room: reaching, hunting, overturning, kicking at them to test for weight.

Only thirteen of the boxes contained anything, and it was noodles, and dried soup. This could not be right. She started again, methodically moving through the boxes. Now and then a sachet dropped from beneath a folded flap on the base of a box, so she would have to pick up and shake each one.

After twenty minutes and many empty cartons she had found only enough dried stuff to last for around nine weeks. And the cans were all gone. She rummaged through the packets and boxes: powdered milk, muesli bars, potato powder, freeze-dried peas. Powdered macaroni cheese.

There had to be more. She started again.

At last, miraculously, one large unopened box, *heavy*. She tore at it, thigh-high brown cardboard, unmarked except for barcodes and numbers. Relief swept through her: it would not be much, but anything to keep them fed would help.

It was not food. It was bandages and dressings, medical tape, antibiotic ointments, latex gloves. A great breath forced up through Yolanda: someone had predicted they would need medical supplies. And here were antiseptic, antibiotics, saline solutions. Splints and cleaning supplies, disinfectant and detergents! Cotton wool, antiseptic, *burn gel*, Burn Aid Film Wrap.

All those months, Hetty's arm gummed sticky with gobs of pus-soaked toilet paper, infected over and over again, so now she would be scarred for life. And Nancy had never, ever gone near this box, not even looked for it. The girls knew they would be left for dead if they could not heal themselves.

Rage pummelled up through Yolanda's body, she could feel it rattling her bones, a freight train of fury charging. She wrenched the packages apart, pulling out everything. She would carry it all back, hurl it at Nancy, stuff the dressings into her nasty little mouth and suffocate her with them, slice these Sterile Carbon Steel Precision Tweezers across her throat.

At the very bottom of the box was something Yolanda recognised from long, long ago. So small and domestic and ordinary she began to cry. It was the shiny pastel plastic packaging of sanitary napkins.

Oh, oh.

All these months, the disgusting shredded rags jammed into your underpants, soaking through. It was worse than anything, the beatings or the hunger, the infections or insults. The wet wad of torn-up tea towels and fraying curtain and threadbare sheet, of old underpants and flannelette shirt ripped into patches and strips, somehow rolled and folded into a horrible lump, forced upwards to mould up into yourself, but the loose stupid bloomers and all of it drenching too quickly, rasping your thighs as you walked, soaking and dribbling. The coppery smell, the chafing hatred in it. Then having to rinse them in dirty tank water in the trough outside the laundry, hang the fluttering rusty flags in the sun. Yolanda had retched into the grass the first three times she'd had to plunge them into the dirty water, clouding with her own trailing mess.

And Boncer and Teddy standing on the veranda sneering down at them, laughing, hands over their noses and mouths, calling out, *Ugh, pigs, shark bait, raw steak. Ah, gross—look out, it's wounded clam.*

Yolanda had once seen an elephant on YouTube, giving birth. The great animal bellowing, swaying, ears flapping in pain as a great silvery pendulum slowly expelled itself, swung and panted its way out, the agony of it, stretching and lowering, and then finally burst onto the ground, exploded, and then torrents and torrents of bloody water came. The elephant kicked and shuffled the lifeless slimy lump over the floor, swirling and sliding in the muck. Wound its trunk around the small body, yanking and dropping until the baby opened its pink yawling mouth and roared. It was supposed to be beautiful, its slipping and staggering to its feet (*So cuuuute! I loove that baby! Wow, what a great mom!*), struggling to live. But then came something

terrible: a huge liverish slide of innards plummeting out. The
zoo people grasped the great meaty fleece of the placenta.
Pulled and stretched out the slippery, shaggy scalloped thing.
Alien, monstrous, female.

Yolanda hugged the squishy mint-green and baby-pink
packages to her chest, squatting in the grief and shame of
how reduced she was by such ordinary things. It was why they
were here, she understood now. For the hatred of what came
out of you, what you contained. What you were capable of. She
understood because she shared it, this dull fear and hatred of
her body. It had bloomed inside her all her life, purged but
regrowing, unstoppable, every month: this dark weed and the
understanding that she was meat, was born to make meat.

But only now it became clear to her that her body and *her*,
Yolanda, were not separable things, and that what she had
once thought of as a self, somehow private and intricate and
unreproducible, did not exist. This was what the footballers in
the dark knew, somehow, when they did those things to her. To
it. There was no self inside that thing they pawed and thrust
and butted at, only fleecy, punishable flesh. Yolanda herself
was nothing, a copy of any other flesh. Meat, tissue, fluid, gore.

She crouched there in the storeroom, rocking and crying
till the snot ran down her face. Eventually she stopped and

sniffed, and wiped her face on her filthy dress. She began unwrapping the pads and tampons and stuffed them, as many as she could fit, down into her dress. Removing any wrapping that would make a noise, inhaling their poetic, pharmaceutical smell. And shoving them down. She would make them last. Those she could not fit she wrapped in the empty plastic and packed them at the bottom of a large dented box marked DRIED POTATO. She shoved other empty boxes down into it over the bundles, pulled it into a corner of the room, covering it with balls of plastic bags.

She threw the medical supplies into the half-full carton of food packages, gathered up the box and walked stiffly, thick with padding, from the room. She locked the door and made her way down the concrete steps, out into the pale yellow day.

• • •

When Verla sees Yolanda's face—when she finally shows up in the ref—it is clear she has been crying. This more than anything alarms the girls, who stare as Yolanda drops the box to the table, moving stiffly as if injured. She has stuffed things down her clothes—food, Verla supposes—but the other girls are not looking at her, only into the box from which Yolanda draws out package after package, slamming them onto the table.

Bandages, sterile clips and safety pins, cotton wool, Dettol. Eye wash, anti-itch cream, *antibiotics*, more and more packets she slams to the table, staring at Nancy all the time.

'Oh!' says Nancy, coming over to see, nervy at the murderous look on Yolanda's face. But then through the door bursts Boncer, Teddy shuffling behind him in downcast reverence.

The girls scramble immediately to sit, bracing shoulders and training eyes on the table, waiting for Boncer's stick to strike. But he says nothing, goes to sit not on his wooden stool by the mantel, instead hitches himself up onto the windowsill and sits there sideways, legs drawn in, curving into the window frame. His eyes are red. He sits there, a thumbnail between his teeth, staring sadly out through the spotted flyscreen, across the land.

Teddy stands a moment with his arms folded, watched by the girls, by Nancy, whose small head jerks as her gaze follows Teddy's movements, alert as a squirrel. He sighs and pads about in his bare feet, unlocking and unclipping the leads, one by one. The girls are motionless, wary, as Teddy unclips them. It is Lydia who stands first, silently sliding from the bench, and stretches her arms above her head, her large breasts rising and falling as her arms slowly windmill. Then Maitlynd copies her, stands and stretches sideways, all of them silent, watching

Boncer for any sudden movement. Teddy just gazes mournfully at Boncer. One after another the girls stretch, for this rare chance must be taken, each bending to touch her toes, or reach her arms backwards, clasping hands behind her back. Eyes always on Boncer, ready for him to strike. But he keeps staring out the window, as if to sea.

Hetty turns her face to the others, eyes wide. *No stick*, she mouths.

It is true, Boncer's belt holster is empty. They look quickly back at Teddy, yawning with his back to the wall, eyes closed. He has no weapon either. He closes his mouth and opens his heavy-lidded eyes, and looks miserably around the table at the waiting girls.

Boncer swings down off the windowsill and strides from the room.

In the silence they stand, straining for clues.

Eventually Nancy snaps into the gloomy air, 'Well?'

Teddy turns his tearful eyes to her. 'Hardings isn't coming.'

They stare at him, confused.

His gaze moves across the girls, one after another, as if seeing them freshly, dreadful. 'We're stuck here,' he says to Nancy, his voice thickening as he realises. 'Like them,' he says, and puts his hands over his face.

• • •

It is the afternoon that everything changes.

Until evening the bowl of land is dotted with the ten wandering girls. Some take off their clothes and trail them in the dirt. Some lie down naked in the sun. Some go in search of food, some for clothes. Yolanda and Izzy and Lydia go down to the dam, lie back in the murky green water, arms outstretched, heads resting in the reeds, pubic bones peeping from the water.

Boncer only sits in the window again, staring out at the dry brown land.

HARDLY ANYONE ventured into the ablutions block anymore. In the beginning they were herded in there by Boncer each morning, and they held their breath and did it because they had never in their lives thought it was possible to shit outdoors. But later, when Yolanda began going off in the mornings and squatting in the grass, they saw the sense of it. Digging a hole in fresh grass with a stick was less revolting, less frightening, than that slimy dark place with its filthy blocked drains and its stench, the brown water dripping out of the tap. When the toilet paper ran out they used newspaper. When that ran out they got accustomed to grass, and were careful with their hands. Under Leandra's army discipline they washed their hands obsessively with squirts of dishwashing liquid, but that didn't stop a wave of gastro coming now and then, laying them all out, vomiting for days.

Sometimes in the early mornings a cry went up in the kennels because Barbs had done one of her deadly farts and it spread, pernicious, under the corrugated-iron wall into the next cell. *Urrrgh, fuck's sake, Barbs,* yelled Maitlynd out of the muffle of hands cupped over nose and mouth, and disgusted mutterings would thread from one dogbox to the next in judgement of Barbs and her lavish, astonishing smells. Barbs would call out, '*I* can't help it, irritable bowel runs in my family!', shrug up beneath the thin blanket and nest further into her bed, breathing in the comforting fruity waft and smiling softly to herself.

• • •

Teddy still spends long minutes inspecting his reflection in the window glass. Sometimes he goes up to the glass and polishes a little patch of it with his sleeve, then settles back to his appraisal.

Most days he displays himself on the veranda, dragging his ratty purple yoga mat around the building to follow the sun, sliding effortlessly from downward dog into cobra and back up, undulating and arching his smooth-skinned limbs. Or slowly, gingerly unfurling into a headstand like a dusty brown flower. The soles of his beautiful feet press together, the legs of his boiler suit fallen down so you can see the perfect diamond made by his muscular calves and thighs.

Another thing about old Hannah was that she was lazy, and she started to get fat. Even though she could have had a good body, she didn't have Teddy's discipline and he couldn't be with anyone who didn't respect their body. Teddy's voice takes on a bitter, angry cast as he describes to Boncer one morning the unceasing nature of Hannah's bitching, through a mouthful of cornflakes—they are sharing the remaining boxes between themselves, and Teddy sprinkles in the last of his psyllium husks. Hannah, he said, suddenly got on his case about, oh, just anything—who did the fucking dishes, who was late with their rent—like some harpy kindergarten teacher. And—*and*, he says to Boncer, the pitch of his voice rising, letting loose a few small spits of milk, she took his really expensive diving booties and threw them on the lawn so her mangy little dog could chew them.

He made her pay him back for them though, *with* interest. He says this with fierce satisfaction, swallowing the last of the cereal and running his tongue around his teeth. He looks across the yellow fields, considering this one victory over whining, bourgeois Hannah, and then yells for one of the girls to come and take his bowl away, holding it out without looking to see who takes it from him. Then he gets up from the table and stalks outside and along the veranda, moving his hips and stretching his arms like some languid jungle creature, towards his yoga mat.

AT THE breakfast table Verla is overwhelmed by revulsion. Maitlynd and Yolanda are scraping their bowls and gobbling. She feels a sudden sweep of appalled, violent hatred for them. How long is it since the girls were all unleashed, since they have been able to come and go from the cells to the ref as they please? How long since Boncer started rationing the food, since she noticed the ceilingful of mosquitoes—last year? yesterday?—and how long has she been feeling so *strange*?

She stares at the two girls across the white melamine plain of the table. Maitlynd's eyes bulge horribly in their pale sockets as she lifts them to look back at her. But Verla is fixated by the blackheads on Yolanda's nose. It is as if she has grown small enough to walk among the greasy tarry surface of these pits in Yolanda's skin. When she thinks of the yellow wax beneath, how it would slowly spiral out, she is filled with nausea and wonder:

how could she ever have thought Yolanda pretty? The fleshy gaping nostrils, her glassy lips. And Yolanda sits there watching her across the table, as if Verla cannot see her ugliness.

She says, 'What's wrong, Verla?' Her huge wet pink lips drawing up over her teeth, her mouth moving like a threat. Yolanda and Maitlynd exchange a glance then, and Verla can smell it. They begin to snicker and the sound of it hurts Verla's ears: she covers them with her hands, which feel very tiny, like a baby rat's claws. She closes her eyes against Maitlynd and Yolanda and their revolting, too-bright presence.

'Please, shut up,' she whispers, but in response they exude a terrible, rotten smell, and she thinks their laughter will shatter the windows.

• • •

Verla hears a swarm of bees coming. Lying in the sick bay she hears it, a light hissing coming from far away. Locusts, from the Bible. In her bed she lies and watches the window; the sky darkens with locusts and the sound grows louder, whooshing nearer and nearer. She pulls the sheet to her chin and imagines the locusts descending, settling over Boncer and Teddy and Nancy like overcoats of turf, like the people of Pompeii, coated in molten lava, stilled by boiled stone covering their bodies.

Boncer and Teddy and Nancy will have their clothes and hair and skin shorn off by the locusts, and be eaten to the bone.

The sound is familiar from long ago.

It is not locusts, not bees or lava or coatings of grass. It is rain.

Verla throws off the covers and runs to the window. She can see flecks of it, sliding silver baubles on the dusty louvres. She hauls open the door, stumbles into the corridor outside the ref where the girls have gathered and are shouting, 'It's raining!' And they pelt along the hallway and tumble onto the long wide veranda and stand there in a row, listening to the rain thundering on the tin awning above them. They stand with their palms stuck out, and some of them lick their hands. Then Yolanda steps down off the veranda onto the dirt, then they all do, Hetty and Lydia and Maitlynd and Barbs and Joy and the rest, thinking come what may they are going to get wet, Yolanda's black curling hair getting soaked, only Verla standing undercover, unable to bring herself over the step because maybe this is a dream. Is it a dream? Her head burns but her heart thumps with the thrumming of the rain and she watches the dusty surface of the dirt eddy into swirls.

• • •

After the rain, Verla goes walking. First she sits down on the veranda edge and takes off her boots. She looks at her once-beautiful feet. They are pale and raw and lumpen, strange unrecognisable loaves, the toes splayed and animal, the nails yellow and curved.

She leaves the boots behind on the silvering veranda boards. She no longer cares if Boncer finds her, bashes her, ties her up. What can he do, other than kill her? Oh, plenty. She does not care. She walks across the yard, past the rusted frame of the old plough, now with weeds growing up between its angles. Picks her way over the gravel on these new, tender, old woman's feet.

It is the grass she wants. Since the rain, the dustbowl around the dam has sprouted and a sheen of acid green has appeared over the ground like an algal slick. But it has stayed, and grown, and now it is there, thick green grass covering the whole bowl of the valley.

She walks towards it, gets down on her hands and knees and crawls in the grass. She sees the fence posts moving. She lies down there, and sleeps in its soft mounds.

When she wakes, her face printed with grass blades, she finds her way to a hillside of scrub. She walks in it like a dream, climbing the slope in the noisy silence. Silty leaves cling to the soles of her feet. There is the patter of wet droplets falling from the gently moving leaves far above. High squeaks and tin musical turnings of tiny birds. Sometimes a hard rapid whirr, a sprung diving board, and a large dove explodes from a vine and vanishes. A motorised insect drones by her ear. She looks upwards, upwards, and sees long shreds of bark, or abandoned human skins, hanging in the branches. The bush breathes her in. It inhales her. She is mesmerised by pairs of seed pods nestled at the base of a grass tree: hot orange, bevelled, testicular.

Then a determined, rhythmic crashing starts up through the trees, through the viney cloth draped all about her like torn circus tents. Her horse! But even before she turns she knows it is not her horse but Boncer. She is caught; it was always coming. She turns as in a dream for him to shoot her, rape her, bludgeon her.

It is not Boncer. The thrashing has stopped; she can see nothing in the silence. Then there it is: the stark, dark narrow face. A kangaroo, straightening itself, growing taller. It watches her, small black paws held delicately before it. They watch each other. Then she sees the other little malleted dark faces: three, six, ten of them—all stopped, all watching her as she slowly perceives their presence. She takes a breath, very still—and then they tilt forwards and make to leap. But then more noise, and more, and all the vegetation thrashes in syncopation; all the bush leaps into shocking life, and she stands motionless, captured, as the blurring streamers of twenty, sixty, a hundred animals overtake her, hurling past. Unseeing, unstoppable, magnificent.

She waits for minutes, an hour, a day after they pass, skin prickling with joyous sweat, her mouth as dry as the leaves.

• • •

It is possible this happened, she thinks in the drenched grubby bedsheets when she wakes. It is possible. She recalls the wind on her face as the kangaroos rushed, and afterwards, when they had long gone, how she and the horse walked together, her outstretched hand flat on its damp, sliding flank as they moved in peace through the dripping, rain-soaked bush.

Nancy sings out from across the room, 'It's the virus! You've got the *contagion*!'

Verla lies shivering with the thumping, thrashing brush vibrating around her, remembering the hidden river she had seen.

Nancy is a shape against the window light now, her back to Verla in the bed, tinkling glass against metal, humming under her breath.

The horse had led Verla to the river, through the trees: a strap of stippled brown leather seen through a gap, catching the sun. Here in the bed now she is so cold she must put her tongue between her teeth to stop the noise in her head, to still the exhausting movement of her aching jaws. She lets her eyes fall closed. If she could get to it again, the river would warm her. It would be warm sand beneath the soft rippled surface, tinted with tea-tree, moving with such ease, such a low quiet glide.

'I'm cold,' she whispers thickly, longing for the sun, that bath-warm tea water. She has said it to Nancy's approaching shape, but Nancy is singing in her high girlish voice and pays no heed to what Verla has whispered, only gropes roughly beneath the blankets for her arm. There is the cold point of a thread pushing past the surface of her skin, a wire or spangle of something hot or cold, and Verla wants to vomit, not knowing if this is relief or death.

Nancy withdraws the needle and presses something to Verla's ice-cold arm, pushes it back beneath the bedclothes. Then the weight of another blanket—so heavy, so welcome but not enough, she wants a steamroller's crush—thumps down over her.

The river is a wide rope of bronze silk twirling, and Verla hammocked inside it. She is a creature of the animals, of kangaroo and horse; she is a little brown trout very still in the water, then a twitch and it's away, somewhere in that channel, scooped along by the river's strong brown hand.

THE JINGLING of rabbit traps came into Yolanda's morning dream, a rhythmic chink of heavy iron, and she felt the beat against her legs, the weight of the dangling black steel fish carried in each of her fists.

It had been a week since Verla began babbling and now lay mad with fever at the mercy of Nancy and Teddy playing nurses and doctors. Whenever Yolanda thought of them with the supplies she had dumped on the table, their gleeful riffling through packets of needles and vials and phials, their searching out poor Verla's faint veins and digging their fingers into her shivering white arms, squirting fluid from needles into the air like they'd only ever seen on *ER*, she went cold and could only think, *Fuck me dead, Verla, I'm sorry.*

She had secretly shared the pads and tampons among the girls. They fell on them like Christmas. But she had also delivered the news of the food, and Boncer began rations, keeping the storeroom key around his neck and fetching each day's meal packages day by day, with extra portions for Teddy and himself, though not Nancy. So this morning when hunger came unfurling again in Yolanda's belly, it was with the sense of a sudden patch of blue sky after rain that she recalled a pair of ancient traps she'd seen hung on a nail at the end of the collapsing woolshed.

She had seen kangaroos here—a family of them, in the distance, every few days when the girls still worked on the road, their slow looping progress across the flat—but not rabbits. But she reasoned there had to be some on this place, its earth so scoured and gouged raw, and if not why were there traps?

She went to Boncer where he was watching Izzy and Joy sorting the packets of food in the scullery. *The sluttery* he called it, about eight times a day, sniggering. They were no longer chained with the leashes, but after his first day of mourning he had grown savage again with his stick, and they were still locked in at night. Yolanda knew he longed to belt her, or worse. When he saw her standing there he looked her up and down, trailed his sticky gaze all over her. She wanted to spew.

'What's up with you?'

'We can eat rabbits. I know where there are traps.'

He looked at her face then, sneering. 'You wanna eat *rabbits*. Like some povo bogan bush pig.'

She folded her arms, covering her povo bogan bush-pig tits, but still he took a good long look. 'It's that or wait till all the food runs out,' she said.

He left the two girls in the kitchen and drew out a lead. He would not let her go without humiliation, at least. He leashed Yolanda up, herded her past the dogboxes to the sheep yards, walking behind her with his stick. She knew how he watched her moving. Same as it had been all her life, but with him her skin crawled more than ever.

She thought of a television puppet from her childhood, a talking bulldozer with a clanking mouth that opened and shut with the sound of hauled metal. The unease that would build in her when the thing appeared on the screen: its loose, unpredictable body, its long swaying neck, the flapping steel mouth. Its driven mechanical power, its imperviousness. If it chose, it could traverse all surfaces—water, sand, rubble, a child, herself, squashed into the gravel—with crushing, inevitable force. And yet it could also wheedle, and laugh monstrously. Her child self understood only that she was compelled to look away when the bulldozer appeared, and that a sour tension in her settled, dissolving, when it was gone.

When they reached the sheep yards Boncer said, 'Get down.'

'What?'

'Get on your knees.'

She closed her eyes. That old sick fear glimmering through her gut, but she would never again submit. She stood. *I will not.*

'Get down,' he said. Standing there with his legs apart, leering at her. Fingers of one hand working at his fly, the other holding the leash taut. He turned briefly, checking again how far they were from Teddy and the house, how alone beneath the high sky and the wheeling birds, and how dark and muffling the woolshed, just there. Licking his dry, flaking lips. He twitched the leash, jerking her towards him.

She tensed, prepared to hurl herself away, took a deep breath with which to scream or vomit or roar or bite. Then she saw Boncer's white-knuckled hold on the leash strap. Saw his skinny pale mosquito-bitten wrists. She saw, finally, what Boncer was: a stupid ugly child, underfed, afraid. She saw his pocked old acne scars.

Pity fought fear.

She heard herself say, 'Don't you ever get sick of this, Boncer?'

Before he could stop it, a cloud of relief, of gratitude passed across him; his eyes watered. Pitiful, pitiful. He stared at her, breathing hard, his eyes red.

'Get on your knees,' he said.

'No,' she said, feet planted.

'*Get* on your knees and suck my cock,' Boncer said, his voice breaking. He was beginning to cry. He yanked hard on the leash, but Yolanda leaned back with her own force, refused to yield. How drab his grey malnourished skin, how sparse the hairs in his mousy moustache, how pathetic his unanswered dating profile, his ugly little neck chain.

'Come near me and I will fucking kill you,' she heard herself say. She had no weapon but still, she had made Boncer afraid. It made her stronger. 'You will never—*ever*—touch me,' she said, her voice low and steady. Shaking her head, leaning back, refusing the tug on the leash. 'You're repulsive, and you're weak. And you're probably getting sick.'

Boncer stood, appalled. Filled with shame, his fly open to show the fading red of his pilled polycotton underpants, the little wet push against the fabric. He saw her looking, shoved a hand down to cover it.

'Let me get these traps or you'll starve with us,' Yolanda said.

He dropped the leash and she stumbled backwards, sprawling as she landed. He raised his stick at her, but still she felt his fear.

'I wouldn't touch you anyway, all the cocks that have been in you,' he spat, as she got to her feet and turned towards the collapsing woolshed, adrenaline surging through her. She knew where the traps hung on the shed wall, knew the trap jaws, knew how they could snap bone. And now, even with Boncer yelling obscenities after her, insulting her body, describing what other men had done to her, crowing all this in his bully's whine, his tears gone, all she felt for him was pity.

It was like a drug.

She clambered over fences, through the pens to the woolshed, and stalked along the side to where she knew the traps would be, dark against the silvery wood. And there they were, rusting steel rags hanging from a nail. Not a pair but six, seven, nine traps. She wiped her muddy hands on her dress.

Boncer watched her, panting, his eyes desperate, red-rimmed. His thin voice was calling out the usual things—but as Yolanda pulled down the traps with a clunking, heavy noise, his voice stopped in his dried mouth. In the iron sound of her traps she knew Boncer heard her new knowledge: she was strong, and he was weak.

She felt the weight of the traps, and all of that—*slut slagheap fat-arsed ugly dog bitch*—was finished. The sound of the traps in her hand was the sound of a battle won, an exhausted peace falling. She held in each hand a drooping bouquet of rusting steel, strode with a heavy step down the rickety ramp. She stepped near to him and twirled her handful, and Boncer flinched at the wide swing of her arm, he had to duck back his head to avoid the bestowal of her pity, the swoop of its rusted chain.

She walked away.

Boncer followed her, not even trying to pick up the leash, as she carried the traps back through the yards, across the combed grassy paddock, up the pink scoured gravel to the veranda. She heard doors open, and girls and Teddy and Nancy stepped out of the doors to see her swing the traps in a dark iron arc in the air, crashing them onto the wooden boards.

Boncer saw the others watching, hurried to catch up, to take hold of the leash and stand over her, to posture and sneer, fondling his stick.

But only Boncer heard her murmured voice.

'That's enough,' said to him softly. 'Fuck off now.' She picked up the traps and slung them over her shoulder, and carried them into the sick bay where Verla lay.

VERLA LIES with her eyes closed against the light, the cicadas from outside crawling in through her ears and nose and mouth, filling her veins and nerves with shimmering fever. It's this that wakes her from her muddy dreams: the cicadas' sparkling threads of pain moving through her body. In the moments she is dredged up from the bottom of her dreams there is not a part of her that doesn't hurt: hips, finger bones, each vertebra in her neck. Her chest is shrunken, thick with cobwebbed veils.

Despite Nancy's attentions, Teddy's too, she feels she will die. Because of them, perhaps. Throughout her sickness she has felt the two of them, their hands, lifting and prodding at her. Their curious, experimental voices. They crouch over the ants' nest of her, poking with a stick, heads together, their breath close and loud. Perhaps they are trying to kill her, and then they leave her to die, and then they come back and rattle little jars and wonder, do more things to hurt her, say mysterious things (*shit really hit the fan, what's emetic, for fuck's sake don't drop that*) over her sinking, failing body, over her vomiting into a dish, over her soft high crying like a sick baby. There is one of Teddy's wide brown hands grasping the back of her head, gripping her jaw with his thick tobacco-stinking fingers, forcing little nubs of something into her throat, and Nancy hissing *no the other way how many what's antipyretic how do you* and sloshing water and making her swallow, each time gasping so as not to drown.

After a time, she knows someone else is in the room, has been there, silent. It makes her afraid, but then she sinks under again. Sometimes she is aware that she is awake, feels her own heavy flesh, this grimy bed.

At last she wakes and her head is opened, there is a space for clarity to come in, as long as she stays very still. Her mouth is dry, and her face is still a thick rubber mask, a moving mask of crawling viral matter. But she can turn her head and see that beside her in a chair is Yolanda, that she has been there all the time.

Yolanda sits by her bed, untangling the legs of some chinking metal spiders, the long limbs of rusted dolls, and now Yolanda's voice murmurs in and out of Verla's fever dreams.

Traps, she is saying. For food. The dolls and spiders are rabbit traps.

She explains them to Verla, lifting, dangling them, into Verla's line of vision. Each one has a long pin for stabbing into the ground, for hammering into hard compacted earth, and attached is a chain. The chain coughs in Verla's chest, she hears it dragging across dry dirt. Then the jaws, *the business end*, says Yolanda, muttering softly.

Verla sinks back beneath the surface, her own jaws shivering. Before she goes under she says a whispered prayer to Yolanda: *Please don't leave me.*

When she wakes again her gluey eyes are clearer. She lies, sticky lips parting to breathe in and out, watching the shape of Yolanda in her dirty grey tunic against the white wall, tinkering on a metal trolley she has wheeled to the bedside. She sits in a chair with her knees spread, boots up on the rungs of the trolley, the tendrils of her traps laid out in the apron of her dress.

Verla lies with her eyes hurting against the light, sometimes opening them to make out what Yolanda describes to her, each pair of tongs ending at a trap, a square mouth with zigzag teeth. A sprung flat plate which, *when fixed, when bloody working*, would trigger the trap and snap shut the jaws. 'Only, fucken thing's rusted shut.'

The crooked teeth knitted up against each other, unmoving. But Yolanda's hands do not stop, covered in rusty grease and dust. She has the pin of a second trap in one hand, gouging and drilling out the rust between the teeth of the first.

Verla dozes into the sounds of clinking and scraping. She has her own work to do inside her fevered mind. Small white stars in the blue dusk, that's what Verla searches out, for even as she has swum into and out of death in this darkened viral state she knows she will kill Boncer. She thanks her sickness for the vision, for her walk in the kangaroo-thrashing bush, her horse, her swim in the warm brown river; all of this has uncovered the mushroom that springs up after rain. She steps through her fever, stalking it, willing herself to find it among the little white pinwheel stars, so delicate, and—

'*Ha!*' Yolanda cries into the quiet air, spitting and blowing at rust, and rubbing the traps with a grubby towel she has found on the floor.

Verla watches Yolanda force the trap's teeth apart and pull at a lacy thread of blackened blood and animal hair, and flick the filigreed bit of it away. Now she pushes the hinges with the heels of her hands, and then there's a scraping noise and Yolanda yelps, jumping from the seat as the trap hits the floor. She grins down at Verla in the bed.

The noise brings Teddy scuffling in through the veranda door. With the light behind him in the fevered airless room, Verla sees Teddy is looking gaunt, his dreadlocks spindling out from his head. He looks as mad as Nancy now.

Yolanda bends down and opens the trap, sets the jaws, looks around the room. A pair of wooden crutches leans against a wall. Yolanda takes one and waves it carefully at the trap: *bang.* The thick wooden foot of the crutch is crushed.

Teddy hisses in fright, jams his hands into his armpits. Yolanda grins, shakes the crutch, and the shattered end of it loosens and comes away. She picks up the trap, inspects the splintered stub caught between the jaws.

'Those things are illegal, you know,' says Teddy.

Yolanda chortles, low and guttural. 'Gunna call the cops on me, Teddy?'

He frowns down and Verla knows he is thinking *ugh* at the two filthy girls, that he is freshly fearful of the lice eggs in their matted hair, of Verla stretched white with illness, of Yolanda and her rusted weaponry. He fears their thin feral bodies, their animal disease and power.

'It's *cruel*,' he says, afraid.

Together they snigger up at him, showing their small grey teeth.

Once, driving with Andrew through the back roads of his electorate, Verla got out to open a gate, and by it was a tree. From the tree dangled a line of strange laundry: the dead bodies of feral dogs. Long, skinny gutted things. Andrew said they'd been there since he could remember, slowly twisting in the air, lengthening or shrinking over the months, feet only just off the dirt. Skin growing stiff and leathery over the years, then dry and light as paper. Verla looks up at Teddy and sees him, and Boncer and Nancy, in a row, hanging, abandoned, from a tree. The rotted leather slippers of their feet almost but not quite brushing the earth. Inside her frizzling skull she says, *You'll know cruel*, and grins.

Teddy steps back from them, shuddering away from their madness and disease, and slams the rickety veranda door behind him.

Verla wants to put out her hand to Yolanda because she knows now that *please don't leave me* was not her own prayer. It was what Yolanda had whispered to her.

Rabbits are long and skinny. Ribbed, fleshless things, filled with tiny bones like a fish. And the tiny bones will break quite easily, and the rabbit skins will be warm.

Verla knows that despite Teddy's scurrying fear it is Yolanda who is really frightened, sitting at her bedside with her murderous traps, frightened Verla will die. She wishes she were strong enough to push her hand out of the bed and reach across the space and say, *Fear not*, for one day soon, when Yolanda comes exhausted into the room, Verla will be sitting up, and she will ask Yolanda to take her elbow and lead her in a slow walk from the bed to the door, across the threshold, step out onto the dry creaking sun-warmed boards, then down the concrete steps and around the compound.

She will have to hold her hand up against the light, too bright, but Yolanda will steer her back into the shade, and she will walk, and Verla will tell her all the things she's seen.

'I left my boots here,' she will say, patting the veranda boards. 'The kangaroos flew past me.'

Yolanda will hold her arm, firm and gentle, supporting the weight of Verla, who will feel like a small bird perching, a small breathless bird, but she will recover. Despite Nancy and Teddy, despite the fever, she will get better.

Now, in the room with Yolanda chinking and scraping her traps, Verla wants to offer her something for this tenderness. She says, her voice thick with spittle, 'I saw a river, Yolanda.'

Her eyes are closed but she feels Yolanda stop and watch her face, which she is making shine with the memory, the glisten of the river. She opens her eyes and looks into Yolanda's deep grey eyes, nodding. 'There's a river. And my horse, that will come for us and carry us out.'

Yolanda gives a small soft smile which means *you poor mad thing*, and says, 'Maybe you better go back to sleep now.'

Yolanda can't believe her. It doesn't matter. For the second time since she arrived here her hand reaches out for Verla's and grips it, gently this time. *She is stronger than me.* The two girls sit together, hands clasped on the thin grey bedspread in the grim afternoon light. Beyond the room and the veranda, out there in the blue dusk, the cicadas shimmer and the mushrooms push their white butting heads against the earth, and the horse treads its great hoofs into the soft black soil.

WHEN THE power goes off during the night, nobody notices. The lights are off, Verla still lies sleeping fitfully in the sick bay, the other girls locked in their kennels. There is no sound other than a final jerk and shudder from the empty fridge.

It is Barbs who discovers in the morning that the kettle won't boil for the instant noodles. The dusty power cord is suspected, but then the washing-up water only runs cold. The fuses are checked, but it is not that. Teddy hurries through all the buildings then, flicking light switches up and down and saying, *Fucking hell, fucking hell.*

As he does it one thought flits through each startled girl's mind: the fence. But Boncer is ahead of them, clipping Leandra to himself and setting off up the ridge.

For four hours the girls wander the paddocks arm in arm, waiting and jittery, picking prickles off each other, passing time by making more lists: of most missed items, what you would do for your bridal shower, songs with the word *love* in the title. Clothes you are surprised to find you miss the most: Izzy's soft cotton yoga pants, Maitlynd's white singlet, Joy's big brother's chequered hoodie (the others smirk: seriously, could you get more bogan?), Lydia's black sequinned boob tube. They go quiet then, for how can she miss that thing, after everything it means, what it led to, what people said? But they have learned enough now, in these months, not to wonder too hard at such things. They let her keep it as a most missed thing.

Teddy goes into his poses on his mat and Nancy crouches beside him, prattling, ignored. From her work with the traps in the sick bay Yolanda sees Nancy through the window, wittering on to Teddy about *her* most missed things: her friends at the hot-bread shop, the roadhouse uniform which was *much nicer* than this, tugging at the fraying cuffs of her boiler suit.

'Do you think we'll be able to get out now, Ted?' she pleads into his silence, staring up at the ridge. 'I hate this fucken place.'

Still Teddy ignores her, slinking through another asana on the mat, exhaling noisily and long, his eyes closed against Nancy's witless voice and her hope.

Yolanda picks at her traps, watching Verla lying pale and feverish on the bed.

After midday a cry goes up: Boncer and Leandra are seen making their way down the ridge. They all gather on the veranda, Teddy and Nancy too. But as Leandra and Boncer trudge closer, red-faced and sweating, both are glum and silent. Some of the girls begin crying, and Teddy's face is taut as Boncer tells them what they don't need to hear. The fence is on some deeper power source, and hums on unaffected.

LIKE FISH scales, like platypus hair, Yolanda thought, except it wasn't river water or rain but the dew that shaped the wet fur into elegant points down the rabbit's long back. Its legs huddled up together for comfort, coiled once the trap had snapped shut and crushed its head. Its long silky feet perfectly aligned, side by side.

Something ancient throbbed in Yolanda. She had trapped an animal, and now she would skin it, and eat it. Somehow.

The air was soft with the peepings and chimes and high whirrings of small birds, insects. Flies. She had searched and searched through the wet grass, trying to find the marker where she had left the trap. Her boots and bare legs, and the stiff bell of her tunic, were wet with the dew. The grass at her thighs rustled like trailing taffeta. A vague dread had risen in her, the cast of a grey cloud moving over her. She trod carefully: what if she couldn't find it, or, worse, set it off herself?

Then suddenly it was there at her feet. She almost stepped on the rabbit's small head with her crusted boot.

'It's all right,' she said in fright, gruffly, aloud to no-one. But it frightened her. The rabbit looked so dead, squashed there. It was she who had killed it.

Yolanda squatted there in the grass beside the trap, watching the rabbit. It must be dead, for there was no possibility of life with the teeth of the trap clamped across its neck, so clearly broken. But she did not wish to touch it, not yet. She watched it for any movement, for its nerves to twitch. Wondering how to get it out.

She examined herself for signs of remorse: she found only some smouldering, some ember.

She put out her fingers to touch its belly. The fur was wet, the body firm; it yielded but did not spring back at her touch. She was relieved no warmth or life met her fingers. She got to work, using her fingertips and a short stubby knife she had talked Teddy into giving her to tweezer the head out from between the trap's jaws.

They had watched her from the veranda setting off: Boncer, Teddy, Nancy. All three were afraid of her now, and hungry with it, watching her out of their hollowed eyes. Boncer kept his distance, but when he was with Teddy he would still yell out at her, call her names. She smiled and knew he was afraid when he grabbed at his thrusting crotch, yelled out *needs this lot in her mouth, permanently, and stitched up* as she passed him below the veranda, her leash-belt hung with traps, clanking and swinging. Swaying already with her armour, smelling of hair and blood.

Boncer whispered things into Teddy's ear that even Teddy turned from in disgust, shaking his head while Boncer hooted. Nancy stood by cackling too loudly, hands in her pockets, all the time waiting for Boncer to glance her way. He didn't. Nancy had taken to twirling up her manky hair in a ratty turban, copying Teddy. When she joined in laughing at Yolanda, saying, *You can smell her rank stinking thing from here*, Boncer only turned and stared at her coldly, then walked away.

Nancy was unravelling. Nancy was crazier now than any of the girls, for Nancy had begun eating up her pharmacy stores in the hours she played nurses on poor Verla, and now she spent her days trailing after Boncer, pale and scratching, pleading for his attention. He ignored her, and once the girls heard him shouting from the other side of the house, *Why don't you just fuck off?* After that Nancy trotted around after

Teddy instead, moaning in her injured, mystified voice, *Why won't he* talk *to me?*

When Nancy cried, Teddy would only roll his shoulders and shrug and flex, then close his eyes against her, bend his scrawny body into a downward dog on the veranda boards, and smoothly breathe, unspeaking, through his poses until Nancy wandered off to sulk and sit cross-legged against the wall. She raked at her scaly arms and bitterly watched Boncer circling the girls, inspecting them from the veranda, staring, teeth nibbling his flaky lower lip.

Crouching here by the rabbit, Yolanda smelled the wet grass, the scent of mud, of decay. Perhaps Nancy was right: perhaps it was coming from her own body. It was hard to tell, now. She prised the trap jaw open with the stick, held down one edge with the side of her boot, and—tugging by the ears—pulled the creature out. When the body came too she was relieved; she had feared the head might come away. Why did that thought sicken her, when she would soon have to tear it to pieces? She gulped the green air and let the trap spring shut again. She turned the rabbit over, pressed the belly, and yellow piss came streaming out of its pizzle, running over her boots.

• • •

The girls were gathered at the kitchen door, peering in at something on the floor by the overturned garbage bin, when Yolanda came in. They looked up, took in Yolanda's bloody hands, the rabbits hanging from her belt, then turned back to the spectacle of Verla crawling in garbage.

'She's after salt, we think,' said Barbs.

Verla crouched in her dirty nightdress, her frail white hands scrabbling through the contents of the bin, strewn in a wave across the streaky green lino floor. Tiny ants crawled over the bits of torn plastic packets and pocked polystyrene cups and bags, the squashed sauce tubs and sachets. And the ants laced over Verla's hands and wrists as she snatched up another noodle sachet, flayed it open with her thumbs and darted her tongue into it, licking and sucking at the coating of yellow powder filmed over it. She tossed that down and took up a macaroni cheese box, ripped out a clear cellophane bag in which a few lurid orange crumbs remained. She licked the silver interior of a soup packet, nibbling into its corners. Wrapper after wrapper she opened and licked, opened and licked and discarded, until Lydia came pushing through.

'I found proper salt,' she said, jerking her head in the direction of a mouldy cupboard across the room. 'There's heaps of it.'

The girls jostled to watch as Lydia worked the lid of the grubby white plastic bottle.

'Don't give it to her!' cried Joy. 'She might have blood pressure! You should of asked Nancy first!'

But the others shouted her down, and Lydia snorted, '*Nancy.*' She yanked Verla's hand open and puffed a little pile of salt into her palm. Verla scoffed it, tongue lapping again into her hand, eyes cast up at Lydia gratefully. Someone else brought water, and Lydia poured in the salt, swizzling it with a fork, and they got Verla to a chair where she sat, gulping, bulgy-eyed and panting. Then they gave her another cup of water, without salt, and she guzzled that too, as Maitlynd held the cup to her face.

'Thank you,' Verla said in a small weak voice. She sat in the chair and lay back against the wall with closed eyes, and the girls all turned to look at Yolanda now.

She stood on the lino, seven dead rabbits hanging from her waist.

In the paddock she had worked out how to force a slit in the back legs with the knife, thrusting the stubby blade through the soft fur, jerking it along the bone. Squatting in the grass at each trap, she unclipped and forced her leash-belt through the slit, then through the trap chains too. By the end she wore a ragged skirt of rabbit bodies and chinking steel traps. Fur, steel, fur, steel. The flesh soon glued to the belt with blood; the heads and ears swung like heavy feathers as she moved.

The girls stood in the kitchen, their feet amid the plastic and tinfoil rubbish and crawling ants. Something moved among them, between them, with this new strange Yolanda, this *hunter*. Delivering bloody flesh to them, bringing warm fur in from the fields. They folded their arms at her in fearful wondering, in hope.

'Where are they?' she muttered, dipping to look for Boncer and the others through the window.

But the girls, gleeful with knowledge, had news of Nancy and Boncer. They looked to Izzy, the proud discoverer, to answer. She tried not to grin.

'Nancy's gone and overdosed. Teddy reckons Boncer found her passed out on his bed.'

Yolanda stared, the girls tittering.

'So they're tryin ta work out how to pump her stomach.'

They cackled—*hope she chokes on her own spew*—as they crowded around Yolanda at the sink. They could smell the mud and death, could smell that things were changing.

Rhiannon helped Yolanda reach around and unbuckle her leash-belt. They watched Yolanda slide the cargo off, jerking the soft bodies to unstick them, forcing them off the end of the leash. She whipped the belt away and reclipped it round her waist. Bloody hand smears down each side of her dress.

The traps pulled away, rabbits in a pile.

'Poor little things!' said Lydia, reaching to stroke their stretched, soft bodies. Then she drew her hand quickly back, grimacing.

Maitlynd had her arms folded tight against herself, but peered down. 'Ugh, I feel sick.'

'Don't be stupid,' Barbs said. 'Tastes like chicken. And I'm fucken starving.'

'Who says it tastes like chicken?' said Hetty, appraising Barbs with a look that said *you don't look starving*. Then she said, 'I'm not eating that. It's disgusting.'

They looked to Yolanda for what to do now.

Yolanda sought out Verla's glance across the room where she sat, exhausted, head tipped back against the wall, forgotten. Yolanda would need to get Verla back to bed—her own dogbox bed now Nancy was convulsing, hopefully dying, in the sick bay. But even half-dead, Verla could manage to roll her eyes about Hetty.

Yolanda smiled down at the animal. 'Don't have to eat it,' she grunted, grasping one of the legs. 'There's always the garbage,' glancing down at the wrappers on the floor. Now Hetty folded her arms, sulking.

Yolanda had no idea how to skin them.

'Jamie Oliver cooks rabbit,' said Barbs dreamily, shuffling in beside Yolanda. 'In his little wooden shed.'

'He's a knob,' said Leandra.

'He isn't!' cried Barbs. 'He's wonderful. And kind. He *cried* on that show about the fat people in America.' She looked to the ceiling wistfully. 'He was sitting on a swing.'

'How'd he cook it?' asked Yolanda, stretching out the first animal, holding it spread-eagled on the bench. She took a breath and began. The others gasped as she jerked a knife along its belly skin. She heard the jagged tearing. It was difficult, clumsy. The knife was not sharp.

Barbs looked down at the torn creature sadly. 'Something, I don't know. Extra-virgin olive oil.' She looked up at Yolanda, tears in her eyes. 'I can't remember!' She turned on Hetty, scornful. '*Italians* eat rabbit.' She sniffed. 'Maybe he barbecued it. In a vineyard?'

They went silent, thinking of Jamie's friendly fleshy face, his butcher's voice saying *darlin*, saying *gorgeous*. His shimmying hips around the bench, flipping and chopping, his meaty hands working on flashing screens, music leaping.

Yolanda grasped the forelegs and lifted the rabbit, silhouetted against the window light. She felt the lump of glowing ember inside her, the ember that had begun to smoulder out there in the field.

The innards slithered out, a neat grey coiled mass, into the sink. She had to reach in and tug at the heart, the lungs, the kidneys that clung to the bones. She felt the cold round wetness of them, tiny beneath her fingers. She plucked them out. Felt her mouth filling with juice at the idea of *meat*.

'*Ughh!*' cried Joy, her hands flying to cover her mouth and nose. Yolanda wanted to fling the organs into silly Joy's stupid pretty face, to smear her with them. She held up her bloody hands and waggled them, making Joy shriek and leap away.

Now to the skin.

The girls suddenly went quiet, and shuffled back as Teddy came into the kitchen. He was pale, looked even thinner. He stood among them, worn out. Staring down at the bench.

'Is she dead?' said Izzy.

Teddy looked at her mournfully, shook his head. 'Really bad, but,' he whispered. 'Looks dead. Just breathing.'

A shudder of disappointment went up. 'Fucking drama queen,' muttered Izzy. They crowded back around Yolanda.

'Skin it,' ordered Hetty, and they all knew it was Nancy they wanted flayed, and Boncer, and Teddy next. They wanted meat. They wanted gore.

Yolanda felt their need as she struggled. She jerked with the knife, ripped and tugged at the fur. But it only came away in shameful tufts and shreds. Her hands were stuck with fine fluff; it floated. She sneezed.

Now she no longer wore her dangling skirt of animals and traps, she had shrunk back into her ordinary self again. Not hunter, only *girl*. But she still smelled the dank smell on herself, and breathed it in. She would do it, become hunter, or animal. She would gather up the gizzards and wear them, wrap herself in a cloak of guts. She knew that across the room, Verla saw. Verla understood.

She turned to Teddy, now slumped against the wall with his face white, his eyes moist. She held the point of the knife at his belly and when he started in fear she hissed, 'Sharpen this.' And because he was Teddy, and both of them were altered, he did.

She tossed the first patchy, balding body aside, took up another.

'Jamie would like this kitchen, you know,' said Barbs then. 'It's shabby chic.'

While Yolanda worked and grunted, the girls looked around at the lead-paint-peeling walls, the dun-coloured cupboards. The battered pans and tins. The cobwebbed slow-combustion stove that nobody knew how to work. 'We need to get that thing going,' said Barbs. Ever since the power had gone out and they couldn't boil the kettle they had been eating the dried noodles raw, and stirring custard powder into cups of dull tank water. Undissolved lumps of powder would burst in their mouths, sticking tongues to gums.

From her chair against the wall Verla slurred softly, 'Need wood.'

They all turned to Leandra, who—Hetty said—*surely* must have learned wood-chopping in the army, somewhere in all that dykey boy-scout camping stuff. Leandra gave Hetty the finger, but shouldered her way outside.

By the last of the seven rabbits Yolanda had got the skinning right: one hard swift motion, like drawing back an arrow. Like cracking a whip, skin departing body in one pulled sock.

There was a pile of soft skins on the bench, and in the sink the pink bodies, curled like unborn babies, cold against the enamel.

Yolanda was warm with exertion. Her hands were slippery. She wiped them again on her smeared dress and then took each skin, stabbed another slit in it, and threaded them back onto her leash-belt with the traps. She left the room, draped in her new costume, her armour of bloody flapping skins and steel, caring nothing for the snickering and whispering that followed her. Verla understood, and that was enough.

THE SKINNED bodies are lining up along the bench as Verla finishes with them, adding one more to the row. Pink, faintly gleaming in the light from the speckled window. Through the window she can see Yolanda coming up from the paddock, a single rabbit dangling from each hand.

Every now and then Verla imagines her old self coming across this scene, across her own present self: her bony ribs, her hair matted, her coated teeth. The filthy greasy calico dress, something out of the nineteenth century. The bucket of rabbit heads beside her: staring eyes, stiff ears, the gory ragged hems of their necks. Her easy familiarity with all these things, as if she was born to this handling of little bodies like slippery new babies, flipping and turning the creatures as casually as the folding of pillowslips. The nimble plucking out of heart and liver and guts.

But might that old Verla, some part of her, have been drawn to this? The taking hold of the rabbit's silky ears, and cutting off the head in one quick motion? The slick pleasure of the guts slithering out? There is some bodily relief in this emptying, voiding. The easeful tumble, the point at which the rabbit stops being itself, begins being food. The guts fall now, glop-glopping into the sink. Verla remembers the old pleasure of shitting, back when there was something to eat other than packet food and rabbit.

She can hardly remember what it is like to sit on a clean white toilet, indoors! Once she got a stomach bug, staying with Andrew in a Guangzhou hotel, and spent twenty-four hours wrapped around the white china bowl. She thought it disgusting, was humiliated at being so lowered, so abject. Having to kneel and put her face into the bowl for vomiting. Now she would happily drink from it.

Here, she now shits outside if she can manage it. A quick rage flares in her, a question for Boncer. The reason for their captivity has a blank clarity: they are hated. But why must they be kept so *dirty*?

She watches Yolanda stride up over the little rise below the veranda, puffs of mist coming from her with her breath. She is the only one who looks healthy: she has blood in her cheeks, is fit from the walking and carrying. Soon she will arrive there in the cold kitchen, warming the air with her freshness and her lifefulness. Together she and Verla will skin the new ones, and Verla will listen to the little grunting sounds of Yolanda stabbing into the soft rabbit belly. There is something intimate about this shared work and purpose.

This is what makes Yolanda strong: the knowledge that without her, without her traps, they would have all perished by now. Only Yolanda is keeping them alive. Through the window she watches Yolanda clump across the yard, the two bodies swinging. She unhooks the traps from her belt and tosses them to the concrete for cleaning later.

Soon two more pink and elongated bodies join the others on the bench.

• • •

Each morning now brings new rabbits, and Leandra's vigil by the slow-combustion stove continues. She sits by the little black cast-iron door, feeding it. The oven smokes intolerably if the door is closed; the chimney is blocked somewhere. But Leandra has discovered that by keeping it open just a finger-width, the flames draw well. She spends her days collecting kindling, dragging larger branches up from the paddocks, jumping on them to snap them into useable lengths.

Leandra crouches by the stove, feeding it tidbits: sticks, splinters of fine dry wood. They gather garbage for her to push in, each piece of plastic wrapper sending out sweet chemical plumes of coloured flame and smoke.

They understand now, after the first week of Yolanda's catch, that the longer you cook the rabbits the more edible the flesh.

Verla thought she would choke on the first mouthful, forced into her mouth by Boncer's long cold fingers. He wanted the meat for himself, she could see his lips wet at the smell of it, they all were crazed for it, leering down at the withered, brown dried-out roasted thing in the pan. But as Boncer had stabbed at it with a knife, Teddy put out a hand to stop him, cried out, 'What about myxo?'

So Boncer turned to Verla, still weak with sickness, every part of her leaning, myxo or no myxo, towards the creature in the pan. During the cooking the rabbit's body had twisted up on its haunches, and it now sat up, like some mummified cat. Verla's mouth flooded for it: this holy thing; protein, life.

Boncer's bony fingers pulling off a wodge of meat with difficulty, clawing and scraping it away with his dirty fingernails, but still she wanted it. He pushed it roughly into her mouth and she closed her eyes for it, welcomed it.

It was a piece of wood. She chewed and chewed but was unable to break it up, her jaw too weak. She opened her eyes, the other girls looking on, swallowing, leaning in, Verla trying harder, pushing the lump to the side of her mouth, gnawing with her molars. She turned it, sucked, Boncer and Teddy and all the girls staring, and then let drop the chewed wodge into her hand, fell back in her chair weeping.

Boncer said, *Fucking useless bint*, and snatched up the dry brown corpse, bit at it to drag off a strip of flesh, flung it back into the pan. Stood with his hands on his hips, staring at the floor, jaw working. But it was no good. He spat it to the ground, a hard pale lump of balsa wood.

Then Barbs's patron saint, Jamie, visited her. 'You gotta *boil* it!' she cried out. 'He did it in, like, some kinda soup! With carrots, and *beer* and shit!'

So each day now it's Leandra at her vigil, kneeling by the stove, feeding it, wiping at it with a dirty cloth. There is Barbs at her big pot on the stove top, her face pink with condensation, peering into the water's rolling simmer. There is Yolanda skinning rabbits in the scullery, tossing them in a pile in the sink and tramping out with a hump of dirty skins in her arms.

And each day it is Verla picking up one pink body after another by its Barbie-doll haunch, and cleavering through bone, imagining Boncer's skinny wrists, his needle dick, each time. So each day there are no carrots and no beer but there is meat and salt and water and rabbit stew. All their hours and days circle the stove and curve towards the stew, and they might be pock-faced and sallow but they are eating, and Verla is strengthening.

Only Nancy still ails, mad from her pills, emerging now and then to scurry and scavenge, red-eyed, drifting, rambling.

The girls sit in the ref with their faces over the bowls and their elbows on the table, rabbit bones in their fingers and juice running down their arms, sucking at the bones like scrawny dirty babies.

But there is Boncer, too, licking at bones, getting stronger. He might have given up Yolanda—she still swings her traps wide if ever he comes within a yard of her or Verla—but now he watches the others with a simmering, vengeful need.

WHAT WOULD people in their old lives be saying about these girls? Would they be called *missing*? Would some documentary program on the ABC that nobody watched, or one of those thin newspapers nobody read, somehow connect their cases, find the thread to make them a story? The Lost Girls, they could be called. Would it be said, they 'disappeared', 'were lost'? Would it be said they were abandoned or taken, the way people said *a girl was attacked*, a woman was raped, this femaleness always at the centre, as if womanhood itself were the cause of these things? As if the girls somehow, through the natural way of things, did it to themselves. They lured abduction and abandonment to themselves, they marshalled themselves into this prison where they had made their beds, and now, once more, were lying in them.

MAITLYND AND Rhiannon made up a sort of tennis-cum-cricket game, using sticks with little broom-like twiggy ends and a ball of wound grasses, that they played every afternoon, squinting into the sun, for weeks. One afternoon they dropped the sticks and fell upon each other shrieking. They clawed and slapped and spat. Nobody knew what the fight was about, but all the girls came running and lined the veranda watching, calling to the two girls—half-heartedly—to stop. Boncer and Teddy hooted and clapped. Afterwards Rhiannon walked stiffly to her dogbox, lay on her bed, and sobbed and sobbed.

PULLING ON her boots, Yolanda heard the soft squeal of a hinge and the muffled judder of a flyscreen door closing. She listened: nobody was ever up at this time. The sky was a deep dark blue, and the air tasted clean and wet. She shifted, yanked on her second boot and laced it quickly. She heard a tread coming along the veranda. Her stomach tightened. Boncer. He had not come near her again but she could feel his hatred, how he watched her through the prism of his fear, how he liked to imagine her suffering. If she were an animal she could forever outrun him, through the grass, across the fields and up along the ridge, the scrub whirring by as she hurtled, fast as a rabbit or a hawk, spinning across the land.

She saw the hawk circling, sometimes, as she approached the traps. Sometimes the bodies had been got at, faces torn away. Sometimes Yolanda carried a stick, and looked up.

But it was Verla who rounded the corner now, picking her way over the boards. She passed by Yolanda's shoulder and stepped down onto the gravel, stood with her arms folded. She was stronger now, almost well again.

'I'm coming too,' she whispered.

Yolanda shrugged the two traps further up her shoulder. With Verla there was no need to speak.

They set off through the wet grass. It had rained all yesterday, and most of the night. The sky lightened quickly as they walked down the bowl of the valley and over to the other side. They would gather the kills from the traps there and reset them all the way back.

They reached the first trap. Yolanda crouched. It was large, this rabbit. It seemed old, its fur matted. It had been in fights, was a warrior. On one foreleg it carried a bald, dirty, scraped patch, as if it had been caught or mauled before, a long time ago, and survived. But it was dead now. Its whole back thigh was crushed in the jaws of the trap, the grass and earth were black with blood. She held its head briefly in her palm, feeling the weight of it and looking into its black eye. *Sorry*, she said to him silently. *Thank you.*

She had found she had begun to feel differently about the rabbits over the past weeks. She looked at their faces first now.

There were some days when she felt a settling, a relief in the belly, when a trap was empty. She looked up at Verla, expecting wincing or disgust, but Verla wasn't watching anything to do with the rabbit or the trap. She was staring away, at the ground. Yolanda cleaned off the trap with some grass, and tied the rabbit (the forelegs on this one, the back were too mangled) to her belt. Its large soft head hung sideways. Verla said nothing, but when Yolanda stood, she was ready to move again.

'Why did you come?' Yolanda said finally. Her voice was dull in her throat; she had not spoken in days.

Verla scanned the grass. Then she muttered, 'Huh!' and darted sideways, diving to the ground. She came up with something in her cupped hand.

Yolanda looked at the white mushroom. She had seen them every time she came out. Now she wondered why she had never picked one. 'It might be poisonous,' she said.

Verla looked down and considered it, her pink mouth bunched. 'I wonder.'

What did she mean?

They kept walking, Verla darting and bending, slowly filling the sack of her held skirt with mushrooms. Yolanda was searching now too, suddenly seeing the little growths everywhere. String-stemmed feathery grey ones, slimy orange shells, and one huge puffed powdery sponge the colour of honeycomb, along with the glowing white bulbs.

'How will you know?' said Yolanda. They worked companionably now that she had handed a sack to Verla for the mushrooms, and shown her how to tie up the rabbits' legs. But Verla did not answer, only smiled her strange smile.

• • •

Back in her dogbox, Verla feels it tingle on her tongue. Russian roulette! But after a while she knows she is conjuring up sensations, imagining them. She is certain the mushroom is not dangerous. It is a disappointment.

She is not in danger. The longer she watches Boncer, the more it is he who is under threat.

THEY ALL had pets now. They were going mad, or finding some strange happiness.

Leandra crouched and coaxed her stove, talking to it, guarding it. Barbs cradling her giant stockpot, washing it and obsessively wiping it clean, carrying it on her hip each morning to the scullery, her heavy metal baby, and plopping in the bodies one two three.

Rhiannon had found the old ute skeleton on the side of the hill, its thin white bones protruding, barely visible among the yellow grasses. Each morning she trudged off up the hill and clambered over the rusted door, in through the space where the roof had corroded away entirely, and into the driver's seat. She sat there with the spider webs and the shit of bush rats or mice, settling herself into the rotted cushion of the mouldy foam seat. Sat there, hour after hour, hands on the steering wheel, staring out through the empty windscreen space at the white sky and the crows. It was her job, each day, to march to the ute and sit there driving herself crazy, and at sunset each day one of the girls would fetch her back, leading her by the hand through the soft dusk. After a while, Rhiannon's face was so sunburnt they made her wear one of the old bonnets whenever she left the veranda. Her hands were as black as soot.

Joy and Lydia—and Izzy too, now—had each other, and their tweezers. They were never apart, one's arm always around another's waist or neck. Grooming each other lovingly, plaiting one another's filthy hair and tying it up with bits of rag, plucking each other's eyebrows so fine they almost disappeared. Sitting in the sunshine, inspecting their legs and pubes and underarms, descending on each enemy hair when one emerged. Smoothing their hands over each other like Braille, eyes closed, to make sure no stray transparent hair escaped attention. Joy and Lydia and Izzy despised the rest of the girls, from their plucked little threesome, disgusted by Yolanda's hairy calves, the faint down over a lip, Verla's *ranga* armpits.

Maitlynd's pet was real: a frog, a great ugly thing that lurked beneath the water tank. She patrolled the windowsills each morning for moths, grabbing and cupping at the live ones, filling the bowl of her skirt with dead ones like petals. She carried them and squatted beside the tank, crooning and whispering as she held them out and the thing darted and gobbled.

Hetty had got religion, and didn't they all have to know about it. 'God has seen us,' she crowed each morning. 'He's *seen* us!' Down on her knees praying in the gravel, 'Lord, may You free us, free us.' Hetty was a dickhead but it was contagious; even Yolanda began to feel something biblical, something destined in this turned tide, this famine ended. As if she with her traps was that Moses, and she had parted the sea and now all that was needed was for them all to walk to safety.

Free us, free us. But once Yolanda was out in the breeze, stalking through the grass for her traps, Hetty's words were nothing but the same old eternal hopeless prayer, as much use as *hey diddle diddle* or *i will survive*. Hetty's prayer was only words, as light and dry as old eucalyptus leaves, crumbling in your fingers.

On her walks for the traps, Yolanda often saw Verla across the grass. Always out first in the dim dawn light, searching out mushrooms in the dew. Weaving across the paddocks, occasionally dropping to her knees with a little cry. Yolanda, crouching and releasing or setting her traps, watched Verla. She knew it wasn't only mushrooms Verla searched out as she stood for long minutes, scanning the hills and horizon. She was looking for that white horse of her fever dreams.

• • •

The song of me rising from bed and meeting the sun. In the soft dewy morning Verla wanders, whispering Whitman. It surprises her, how much she remembers of the book he gave her, the lines rustling from her lips as she walks, searching for mushrooms, each morning. She knows by heart, of course, those early words he had murmured, nuzzling, when she thought she would burst like fruit from the heaviness of all that fermenting desire. His, her own. *You settled your head athwart my hips and gently turned over upon me.* She trudges over the grass, feels the working bones of her own narrow feet in the cold leather boots. *And parted the shirt from my bosom-bone, and plunged your tongue to my barestript heart.* The currawongs dropping their silvery notes. Verla feels the old slow heat rising in her with the recitation. That 'stript'. Before him she had never known that even spelling could be erotic. There are cobwebs starred with dew everywhere here in the wet green-gold grass. *And reached till you felt my beard, and reached till you held my feet.*

But now, the grass brushing her calves, soaking the hem of her tunic, and the sun softly warming the earth, it is not plunging tongues and stript chests (but oh, the sweet open planes of his chest, she could cry for it, and did) but other, surprising fragments, things she has not known she knows, that come to her. *And mossy scabs of the wormfence, and heaped stones, and elder and mullen and pokeweed.*

She sees, in the little well between tussocks, a swell of fresh white humps, moves to it. *Alone far in the wilds and mountains I hunt.*

Bending, she grasps the root end of the largest mushroom and lifts it to her face. It smells of earth and dankness, almost human. She runs her fingertips over the soft frills beneath its hood. It's not the one she wants, probably. But still. She drops it with the other, smaller ones into the pockety gloom of the tea-towel sack.

The white of the mushroom cap is the same dusky, chalky white of the horse she had seen in the night. And of the unicorn, in Paris.

In the Musée de Cluny they stood before the tapestries, his thumb stroking hard, desirous, over the bones at the base of her neck. She leaned back into that rhythmic stroking, feasting her own mind and senses on the wondrousness of the tapestry. Shocked at the effect of these hangings on her when all the other old dead things he showed her only bored her, or confused. But here, the reds and bronzes, the small playful rabbits, and the monkey burying its little face in flowers. The virgin holding fast to that unicorn shaft, Verla knew what that felt like in her hand (she was never a virgin with him, but he liked pretending) and back at the hotel they turned over and under one another in the streaming sunlight, and the woven threads of the tapestries all merged inside her: the poetry, the tastes, the smells and sounds and visions, the flowers and harp and My Only Desire and the Body Electric, and Verla knew her life had truly begun.

That was long ago now.

She moves through the grasses, her body brought alive once more by this memory and the resurgent knowledge of what separates her from the others. She is not like them. She was tricked, yes, but not by him. He did not exploit her, assault or paw at her. She was worshipped, and wanted every bit of it. *The curious roamer, the hand, roaming all over.* Even after all this time, she knows it is true.

Bodies, Souls, meanings, proofs, purities, delicacies, results, promulgations. The denial forced upon him (he cried, he said, typing those words). Her fingers are cold, now, in the damp morning air. She pushes her fists into her armpits as she walks and searches.

The *relations* he *did not have*. But he did, fervently, and so did she, and somewhere he is missing her, sick with worry, wanting her back, whispering, *Sorry, I'm so sorry* with all his barestript heart.

HETTY WAS a fucktard, and yet it was stupid, ugly Hetty who gave Yolanda the secret to her pets: the skins.

'*Brughn*,' Hetty grunted one morning, through a mouthful of dried soup. She was standing, doggedly munching the grey dust, making slop and paste in her mouth, steaming breath in and out of her nose as she mashed.

Yolanda ignored her, concentrating on holding aloft another steaming boiled skin, dripping into the metal bucket. It might have been the rank smell of the failed skin, or it could have been Yolanda herself, her own smell beginning to merge with the animals', that made the other girls hold their noses and make noises as they shoved past her.

Hetty swallowed finally and said stickily, audibly this time, 'Brain. Should use that.'

Yolanda looked at her. Hetty picked at the grey sludge in her teeth with a dirty thumbnail, then ran her tongue over them, wiping her hands down her dress. Her cardinal used to watch that never-ending show about building houses, and then another one with the same Pommy dude who made his own little shed by hand. He cured a deerskin with its own brains, Hetty said. For why, who the fuck knew.

'Mashed em up,' she said. 'Rubbed em in.'

Yolanda had been trying all sorts of things. Boiling water, salt, vinegar, none of it working or stopping the hides from curling and hardening in their matted stinking state.

The brains worked.

The first time, taking that fine little head in her hands, she felt a reverence, a loss. It was like a bird's head, almost. She held it tenderly, the small closed face, ragged and bloody at the roots of its neck. But still: she scored the thin furry skin between the ears, and separated sideways with her thumbs, revealing the cold private slit of bright white bone beneath. She sat on the wooden veranda step, lowered the sleek dome of the head by its ears to the step below, lodged it between her feet. Took a knife and a mallet and *whack* as she whispered, *Sorry*, and then a clean split in two. The brain lay there, a gizzardy lump. She fingered it, plopped it into a bowl. Did not look at it when she made the first pushing, squashing mash, felt it burst and ooze.

She soon grew accustomed to it, and the wet raw gloves of the skins became her pets. The other girls, except Verla, avoided her even more now she took a hideous sensual pleasure in it, comforted by the rhythms of the tasks: the skinning and scraping off of fat and flesh. The dipping and boiling and stretching, the salt scrubbing, the slippery sliding of her brain-wet fingers, shampooing the smooth hides with the pulp. She felt she was giving love, in this emulsion. Massaging in tenderness and thanks to the small creatures through the inside of their skins.

Probably she was going mad. Verla would sit with her and tell her again about the paintings she had seen in Paris with that politician mongrel. Verla, poor thing, still believed in him. Yolanda didn't argue as Verla carefully talked her way around the fact that she thought she was better than the rest of them.

Verla's voice glittered when she talked about the paint on the pictures, how it piled up and sparkled under the lights of the galleries. How the actual curls and lumps of the paint made the picture dance, made wet oily stuff into cornfields and hospital gardens and crabs and sunflowers. It wasn't the image but the *paint*, did Yolanda see? No, she did not see, Yolanda . . . only sometimes as she listened, watching her own fingers making a moussey lather of the brain mess, she thought she *could* see it, the light catching the whorls of the soft peaks on the brain suds.

Sometimes the two girls looked at each other, and Yolanda felt understood. To Yolanda, Verla *was* better than the rest of them, better than herself.

And then Verla would get up and take her glittering paintings and her strange filthy poetry back into the kitchen and chop up rabbit meat to eat. Verla, like the others, cared nothing about the pelts, they slavered only for meat, lined up along the bench, tugging and hacking and tearing with their blunt knives at the thin skinless bodies.

But for Yolanda, the skins were everything. So light, so easy to destroy—burning the fur away too soon, not spreading the brain mix smoothly enough, so they dried and hardened in the wrong places. At night she would tug at their edges, pulling and stretching so they softened and silkened, the miracle of the stiff dead thing slowly turning to softest chamois in her hands over the weeks.

Soon she would not be seen without two, three attached to her. Tucked into her waistband, flapping as she moved. Another, raggedy strip wound around her arm, tied there. Later, a kind of neckerchief, rabbit legs made into strange bonnet strings.

She moved, and the skins drooped and swayed, bulking out her figure as she stalked the paddocks in the dawn.

She made drying racks for the skins on the south side of the veranda—too much sun was ruinous; it must be shade and gentle, steady warmth. She now carried skins with her everywhere, always smoothing and grasping at some piece, softening it over a chair back or scraping the fat and tissue away with one of the small sharp stones she carried now in her pockets.

Some of the girls said Yolanda had gone crazed, but she knew she was sane, and getting saner. Weren't they all stronger, now they were eating meat? Wasn't there industry now where there had been only captivity?

Yolanda felt some primitive strength mounting as she scrubbed and stretched, as she marched the paddocks and set and sprang the traps. It was a vigour to do with air, and the earth. Animal blood and guts, the moon and the season. It was beyond her named self, beyond *girl*, or *female*. Beyond human, even. It was to do with muscle sliding around bone, to do with animal speed and scent and bloody heartbeat and breath.

Covered in the reeking skins she crouched sometimes among the tussocks, watching Boncer looking for her and not seeing. She was becoming invisible.

IN THE meat locker Verla closes the door and hooks the latch. Only Yolanda knows about the mushrooms and she is at sea in her kingdom of rabbits, devoted, uncaring.

This is where Verla brings her mushroom catch: her laboratory. Nobody comes here, to this dark airy room of tattered flywire panes and a pressed earth floor, set away behind the old concrete laundry in the shadow of the water tank. If she sniffs the smooth curved surface of the butcher's block, she can smell the greasy, rank odour of old meat. How long is it since the skinned bodies of sheep and cattle were dismembered here, cleaned of the last tufts of wool and shreds of hairy skin, hacked into joints and hung? The old ice chest with its hoary galvanised-metal face, its bulbous hinges, is just a cupboard now.

She goes to the wooden crate hidden behind the ice chest and pulls away the sack covering the contents, her drying mushroom haul, and tumbles her day's catch into the crate. It is half full now. She drags it across the floor and reaches into it, drawing out each foamy weightless thing one by one, laying each one on the broad surface of the butcher's block. Once again she arranges them in rows, to inspect and categorise, learning the shapes and markings, the subtle differences in smell. The wide flat brown ones are easy: portobello, simple field mushrooms. Dull to look at, but still she likes to run her fingertips along the under-frills (a memory of Andrew racing through her mind with the shirred-satin flip-flip-slip beneath her touch).

She puts those to one side. The others are the ones with possibility, the ones to test. There are the tiny, delicate, silver pinwheels. These are so fine they almost dissolve at her touch; she has learned to pick them at their stalk using two fine twigs as pincers. They melt on the tongue, and beyond a slight bitterness, nothing. There are the ridiculous fairytale ones, bright red with white spots, and the narrow tawny hooded ones, the monks' hoods with slender pale stalks. Another set of bulbous lurid yellow domes with stained, meaty stalks. When she turns these over the undersides of the hoods glisten with sticky honeyed stuff. It's this one she must try today: surely there is promise in this acid yellow, those gouts of bloody mould.

She dabs a finger to the honeydew and puts it on her tongue. Now she must wait, and time any response. She scratches a number and a symbol for it into the dirt floor beside the ice chest, alongside the rest, and begins counting the seconds. While she waits she lays the mushrooms out in rows by shape and colour and size, keeps counting the seconds.

After five minutes, nothing. She has to give it an hour before she can leave, forty-eight hours before she knows for sure. She paces and circles the meat locker, thumbnail between her teeth, waiting, counting, marking off the minutes in blocks of five, then ten, on the floor.

On two days there have been glorious hallucinations—rippling, breathing, magnificent—but only with one kind of brown monks' hoods, and she has not found any more. Another time she fell asleep for almost half a day, and was visited again by the little brown trout from her sick-bay fever. In the dream her sleek, speckled fish body was weightless and at peace, suspended in water, hovering.

Afterwards she woke dry-mouthed, terrified of discovery, but nobody had come. She brushed the imprint of earth from her cheek and stumbled back to the dogboxes. None of these effects are what she wants. But she is grateful to that little brown trout within herself, gathering stillness. Sometimes she takes it with her into sleep.

She paces, waits; an hour passes with no effect. She grows reckless. She crumbles off a thumb-sized chunk of the yellow hood and chews it (ugh, so *bitter*), swallows it down. Starts counting again, and collecting and storing away her hoard once more.

Perhaps she has already begun hallucinating, perhaps some of them send off psychoactive gases, else why does she spend so many hours here in the damp sporey gloom, walking round and round a butcher's block staring at fungus, so drawn to them, so loving? Because Yolanda may have her rabbits, Hetty her religion, they may all have their pets, but only Verla has a plan. Observe, identify, classify. Preserve, conserve, bide your time, wait your chance. Then: act.

Sometimes in the night she has lovely visions: Boncer crawling, maimed, on the floor while Yolanda and Verla stand above him, their arms folded, unmoved. He scuffles, convulses, begs things of them. Debased.

But today will not bring those visions. She still feels absolutely nothing. And she knows more nothing will come on her in the night, or the morning, and the raucous yellow mushroom will prove as fraudulent and harmless as the rest.

IF LYDIA had a baby she would call it Dakota or Siena. Or Judith, after her grandmother. Some of the girls were lying on the western veranda boards in the late afternoon, warming themselves in the last thin pale strip of winter sun before the day's end. Dakota was nice, they agreed dreamily. What if it was a boy? said Maitlynd, but Lydia wrinkled her nose. 'I'd *abort* it,' she said.

Leandra, who lay on her back with her knees bent, arms stretched behind her head with the backs of her hands against the soft silvery boards, snorted. 'You wouldn't know till you had it, you idiot.'

Lydia rolled onto her stomach, looked along her arm, lining it up with the floorboard edge. 'I would. I'd have one of those scan things, and if it was a boy I'd get rid of it.'

Across the way Teddy and Nancy came down the storeroom

steps with their arms full of boxes. None of the girls had been allowed in there for weeks; they had no idea how much food was left. Nancy chattered away at Teddy, who only muttered in reply. Teddy had begun to disappear periodically with Nancy to the sick-bay medicine cabinet, returning to the rabbit dinners with a glazed look, his lips wet and red.

The girls watched how Teddy used Nancy. He was disgusting, like all men, they agreed. It was men who started wars, who did the world's killing and raping and maiming.

'Imagine if women ran the world,' breathed Izzy.

There was a silence.

Rhiannon murmured, 'But I *like* men.'

All faces turned to her, so she added quickly, 'Not *these* ones, obviously.'

'Imagine this place if it was just us,' said Barbs.

The others considered this, in the quiet. Eventually Joy's small voice said, 'There'd still be Nancy.'

'And Hetty,' said Maitlynd.

They shuddered.

A flock of white cockatoos arrived, landing noisily down on the flat, the white line of them billowing and settling like a thrown bedsheet.

'I miss peas,' said Rhiannon mournfully. She used to eat them in front of her screen from a cup. Still frozen, with a teaspoon; or if they clumped together, she would lift a chunk and bite into it, the ice deliciously mashing with the peas, creamy in her mouth.

• • •

One frosty morning Teddy was seen slipping out of Nancy's room, buttoning up his boiler suit, and later the girls heard Boncer and Teddy shouting from deep within the house. After that, Teddy let Nancy take his arm when they emerged from her room, glassy-eyed, let her lie beside him while he sunned himself on the yoga mat. They slumped together against the wall in the pale winter sun. Now and then Teddy would rouse himself, go for long walks alone, but each night he would return to Nancy and her pills.

Boncer grew nastier. He still watched Yolanda with hate-filled lust from the veranda boards as she trudged the paddocks, but she always carried her traps, and he knew better than to approach her. Instead his hatred of her, his need, spilled out onto the others. He would slink up behind them with his stick, thrust it between their legs to make them jump, run it up their necks as they ate, making them shrink from it. Sometimes

Teddy or Nancy half-heartedly pulled him away, slurring, *Come on, mate*, but they all knew it was only a matter of time.

It was Leandra who found a way to remove the bolts from their cell doors and fix them to the other side. They locked themselves in at night now.

• • •

They are at the bench in the scullery, scraping fat off the skins, when Hetty says slyly to Yolanda, 'Why don't you?'

When the other girls realise what she's talking about they stop what they're doing, take a breath and wait for Yolanda to turn on Hetty. With her rusted steel, or maybe simply one of her strong filthy paws, grasping Hetty's throat.

Yolanda rarely speaks anymore; occasionally she is heard mumbling something, or grunts some instructions to Verla, but to the rest of them she says nothing. Now she straightens up from the corpse on the bench before her and stares at Hetty. Verla is reminded of the kangaroos, when she and Yolanda sometimes come across them by surprise. They grow taller, stock-still, staring for one long slow minute before turning and leaping casually away, the undergrowth cracking around them. In this way Yolanda turns from Hetty's cunning little smile now, and rips her knife into another stiff furred belly.

Hetty is nothing but a curiosity, a whining mosquito. Yolanda has work to do.

The girls return to their scrubbing, but Verla watches them sneaking glances at Yolanda, assessing her now as Boncer might, as Hetty does. The strong jaw, the high noble forehead. Her wide, full mouth, the heavy-lidded Cleopatra eyes. The long, creamy body, somehow in her tatters of rabbit skins even more majestic. Her shorn hair has grown back in an oily black pelt. To keep her ears and neck warm in the early mornings in the paddocks she has fashioned a lumpen furry scarf. Its hard, unevenly tanned hide makes it sit high on her neck: a collar of fur that further emphasises her royal bearing, the clarity of her fierce grey eyes.

Hetty hasn't finished, though. 'You could get privileges,' she says. 'He'd do whatever you wanted.'

Yolanda speaks then, her voice husky from lack of use: 'Over my dead body.' Cleavering through bone.

Hetty taunts, 'He'd probably like that even more,' and a snigger ripples around.

Izzy leans in the doorframe and says plainly to Yolanda, 'But it's not like you haven't done worse, though, is it? Nobody heard you complaining when you did it back then.'

Verla sees a cloud of terrible pain cross Yolanda's face, then vanish. Nobody moves or speaks. Izzy looks frightened, only now realising what she has said. Yolanda behaves as if she hasn't heard, working away at the rabbit carcass, ripping skin from flesh, breathing steadily in and out. But Verla feels Yolanda's heart pulsing in her own chest.

At last Yolanda turns to Hetty and croaks in contempt, 'You want privileges? You do it.'

All the girls look at Hetty. Nobody has thought of this, that Boncer might accept anyone else. Especially Hetty. Even she appears not to have thought of it. But Verla sees it dawning on her, with the knowledge that Boncer is growing desperate. Hetty considers, rocking on her feet, staring out the window above the bench. She pushes past them, through the ref and off down the veranda steps.

• • •

Later, on the gravel, Hetty announces, 'I'll do it.'

Nine girls stand around her: spotty little Hetty, who lifts her chin at all of them, suddenly powerful.

'Really?' Leandra looks at her in disgust, but relief is also moving through them. If Hetty does it, if Boncer will have her.

'I will need certain things.' She speaks haughtily out of her stumpy little face. The thick lips, the pale lashless eyes; she is purposeful now as she has not been before.

Yolanda's chest, crossed with furs, rises and falls. She turns to the others, 'Give her what she wants.'

The other girls begin muttering indignantly—who made Yolanda the boss of everyone?—while Hetty chants a list. But they think of Boncer's spindly fingers crawling over their own skin, his foetid breath in their mouths. If he will be satisfied with Hetty . . .

Verla looks up to the veranda, to see if they are watched. They can hear Nancy's voice wheedling at Teddy from inside the house, and she knows that behind some darkened window Boncer waits.

Yolanda is already sitting in the gravel, wrenching off her boots and swapping them for Hetty's with the one flapping sole. Some of the girls direct bitter looks at Yolanda as they yield to Hetty's demands.

By the end Hetty wears the least rotted tunic, the best boots, has negotiated more food and less work. She stares around her in triumph, examining their clothes, searching for something else she can claim. She finds it.

'And a doll,' says Hetty.

For a moment they stare at her, not understanding, all their faces turned to her in the silence, the sky looming white above them. Boncer has appeared up at the house, leaning on the veranda rail. Hetty's neck flushes, a peculiar mottle of white and red. Nevertheless she stares back at them, meeting all their eyes, and they know she means it. She wants a doll.

Barbs speaks first, in disbelief. 'What, to *play* with?'

'Yes.'

'Like a baby,' says Rhiannon, baffled.

Yes. Hetty isn't flushed anymore. She stands defiant before them, in her new clothes, hands on her round little hips, shoulders back. 'A doll. Or I won't do it.'

There is a bewildered shiver, a *where-does-the-stupid-bitch-think-we-are-going-to-find-a-doll* murmur, but Boncer has moved to the top of the steps. He knows something is happening. He sees them watching him and grins horribly, planting his feet apart on the floorboards, fondling his stick.

'We will make you a doll,' says Verla.

'By tomorrow,' Hetty says.

'Oh my god, you must be joking,' says Lydia.

'Tomorrow,' Verla says.

Hetty turns to face the veranda.

COULD YOU be grateful to someone you despised? Yes you could, and Yolanda was. When Boncer had appeared on the veranda there was a tightening of the air. The girls went silent, and someone—not Yolanda, though she craved to do it—pushed Hetty forwards. Hetty, poor stupid little Hetty, stood with her hands by her sides, clenching and unclenching her fists. Did Boncer know at that moment, did he understand this offering, appeasement? He turned his stick slowly in his palm.

Then Yolanda, too, turned away and left Hetty there to be picked over. Boncer leaned against the veranda post, one foot crossed over the other, confused, inspecting Hetty where she stood below him on the gravel. She waited, lumpish and squinting. As the girls hurried away they heard Boncer snarling in outrage, '*This* ugly dog? Call the fucken RSPCA!' And then his voice went low and horrible, saying things to

Hetty they were glad they could not hear. They scuttled to their boxes, ashamed, and slammed their doors.

In her cell Yolanda took up a fatty uncured skin from the bad-smelling pile and sat on her bed, scraping at it across her knees. Images came and went—a gruesome naked Boncer, his probing stick, Hetty's clenching hands. She let them fall through her mind and quickly away, a hard scattering of marbles. In the clattering were things that had come to her in dreams here: a barking dog's vicious mouth, a flapping of wings, a body staked to a road for the vultures.

They had offered Hetty up to what should have been Yolanda's fate.

In their own boxes the girls were first silent, waiting for shrieks from up the hill. Then someone said Hetty was their virgin sacrifice and someone else snorted *hardly*. The sniggering passed from cell to cell. They would not be sorry. The silly bitch had offered herself.

Yolanda scrubbed and scrubbed, felt again the dissolving collapse of her own rib bones, the torrent of relief beneath them when Hetty had said, *I'll do it*.

The girls' sniggers stuttered, petered out. There was an accusing silence. Yolanda felt it through the iron walls. Then Verla called out, 'We have to make the doll.' This was met by another silence, which this time meant: Make it your fucking self.

Yolanda could not stand thinking of Hetty anymore. She took up her traps and set off, the corrugated-iron door of her box crashing behind her.

It was beginning to spot with rain, the sky lowering. Yolanda marched, her traps bumping against her thighs, thinking of the animal waiting in her trap, its cold blood congealed on the black iron teeth. In her head she counted the uncured skins drying outside the kennels. She felt her own breath drawing into her lungs, pulled the skins and collar closer about her to keep the rain from drizzling down her neck. It was getting colder.

At last she came down the balding slope and found the trap, near an ancient half-buried rotting branch. In the trap a large buck, brown-eyed, its neck crushed, stone-cold dead.

She squatted to release it. She put her fingers out to the soft fur, but something stopped her. It was the same as all the others, but now she was halted for a moment by its particular beauty. The carved elegance of the ears. The rounded contours of its body, the subtle tortoiseshell pattern of its fur now powdered with a fine crystalline mist of rain. The stark white of the tail, and the resignation of its glossy brown eyes.

Then Yolanda thought she heard the faintest, muffled whine. She started, looked behind her across the knobble of ground. It took her a few moments to see, a little way off, tucked between two deep tussocks, a rabbit hunched, quivering.

In all this time she had not seen one alive, close up. She crouched, watching in silence. Surely it would see her, dart away. The rain began to thicken the air. She shifted on her haunches, to show herself. She thought the rabbit saw her—it must have—but it only shivered more, hunching into a ball, seemed to convulse. It was sick.

She shuffled closer. The rabbit knew she was there, hunkering down in its jittering body. She heard again the faint, faint sound. It was in pain. The rain began coming down properly now, dripping down Yolanda's nose, running inside her furred collar. Somewhere back there Hetty was curling under Boncer, offering herself to his foul breath, his cold urgent grasp.

A slow throb rolled through the rabbit's body and Yolanda suddenly understood it was giving birth, or trying to. In the cold and the rain. The rabbit babies, the kittens, would die out here, unprotected.

Yolanda's hands reached and grasped hold of the rabbit. She gathered it up, now kicking and convulsing, and thrust it inside her tunic, between her body and the cloth, whispering, trapping it. No kittens yet lay on the earth where the animal had been. She would warm it with her own body, calm it. But the rabbit kicked at her stomach, its fierce claws scratching. Still, she would not yield; she would bring it to a safe warm place. She managed to stand unsteadily with her screeching, jolting cargo, winding her belly skins tighter around herself, pressing the animal to her. (Was Hetty pressed close? Was she repulsed, did she kick?) But the skins, the skins, she urged it; couldn't it smell its own kind? She was its kind.

She began walking, talked to it, *You are safe, you are safe*, kept walking. It kicked and shrieked but Yolanda was the protector in the driving rain, walking and whispering, *Be calm, be calm*, and slowly she felt the rabbit's cold body warming, quieting. It struggled less, only now and then a convulsive kick. *Come on*, she whispered, *I'm sorry*, and, *Soon you will be safe*, and the pulsing body eased and calmed with the motion of her walking. She rounded the hill, convincing, willing it, and felt the pulsing of coming life. Then oh! a throb of birth, she felt it against herself, a wet warm slide. It was coming, it would be safe. Another nuzzling wet slide, and she walked so tenderly, curving and cupping the mother and the soft wet bulbs of the babies with her arms and body, and it was her own live born she carried, she was animal now. Yolanda was a creature moving as she should, held to the earth with purpose and gravity, labouring in the work of birth out in the darkening fields beneath the raining sky.

AFTER YOLANDA bangs out of her dogbox and storms off across the paddocks, the girls stop talking and the silence returns. Verla lies on her bed. The light outside is deepening and the temperature has dropped; soon the air will be bitter and cold, and there will be rain. Verla does not think about Hetty or Yolanda, but rain, and the white heads of mushrooms nudging upwards through earth.

In a moment there are footsteps through the grass towards the dogboxes, and a faint panting. It is Boncer leading Hetty to her cell. A whisper starts up through the walls as they hear his tread, the keys jingling from his belt, and they understand that he wants them to hear what he is going to do. They stay in their kennels but open the doors a fraction to watch Hetty coming down the corridor. They cannot abandon her for this last procession. She shuffles, flat-footed, behind Boncer, clipped to him once more with the lead; he owns her now. The damp air wafts up as they pass, and a couple of large paint shreds drift to the boards in the wake of this macabre wedding march.

As she passes Verla's door, Hetty meets her gaze through the crack, and Verla knows the other girls in their cells are waiting and watching too.

She brought it on herself, they repeat to themselves. They silently spit her name, call her a stupid slut for giving herself up. She made her bed.

After they pass, Verla edges through the doorway to watch Boncer lean his shoulder into Hetty's dogbox door to open it, go inside. At that moment Hetty turns and stares up the corridor to all the girls. Her lips are taut with fear. In this moment her mind is changing, this is the plea from her eyes, but it is too late and she knows it. Boncer yanks on the lead and she jerks forwards from the waist, and stumbles into the cell, out of sight. The door closes with a heavy shunting sound.

There is a thundering as all the girls burst from their doors and scramble out, away, up the hill. They will not listen to what Hetty has brought on herself.

They clamber to the veranda and huddle, out of the rain, idly scanning the paddocks for Yolanda, not seeing her grey-furred figure moving softly between the dead grasses in the grey light. The rain comes harder now, blowing in drifts beneath the iron roof, churning the gravel into mud. The girls stand, cold and damp, crossing their arms for warmth, waiting for Hetty's bargain to be done with.

• • •

When Hetty and Boncer come out of the kennels the storm is over. The sunlight comes slanting from between the black clouds, moving swiftly across the land, lighting up the row of girls on the veranda, waiting. Boncer comes first, then Hetty. Hetty knows she is watched; she glances up at the girls, and straightens her spine. She wears her nightdress—she is barefoot, padding over the muddy wet grass—and carries a bundle, her tunic wrapped around what must be Yolanda's boots, perhaps her underclothes. She is Boncer's new pet and he is taking her away. She performs her walk, her head high.

But Boncer is the surprise. Boncer is altered. He blushes as he nears the veranda. There is an air of triumph about him, but also something else: surrender. He holds the leash in his hand as he leads Hetty—she is no longer clipped to him—and his stick swings by his side, untouched. As he reaches the steps he pauses and holds out his hand. But Hetty shakes her head, swiftly, not looking at him. She will not be seen holding Boncer's hand. She is not that stupid.

They step up the stairs and into the house. Hetty sweeps one look around at the girls, lingering on Verla, before turning into the doorway.

They stand, dumb. But Verla knows what Hetty meant.

'We have to make the doll,' she says.

It will be a thing of pillows and bootlaces, bottle tops and socks. Dead grass for stuffing. Feathers, bark, reeds, plastic bags papers wire rope anything. Go.

THE RAIN eased, then stopped. Yolanda walked and walked, whispering, carrying her babies and their exhausted mother, who breathed softly now. Yolanda's clothes and the skins made a pouch for the nubbling wet creatures, and the heavy, triumphant weight of the mother rabbit. No more shivering. She was sleeping, in the cradle of Yolanda's animal self.

Birds had started up in the newly light afternoon.

She climbed carefully down the ridge. The others could make their doll but Yolanda would bring Hetty these real babies to pet, to hold against her cheek. She would feed and stroke them and this would feed the new self she must become, the fine wet membrane that must grow over her, like a caul. A new skin over the old wound that Boncer filled with his decaying self. It was possible to make yourself new, this was what Yolanda had discovered. This was what she would explain to Hetty, and show her how, when she told Hetty to close her eyes and hold out her hands and she set into them the soft, downy weight of such perfection.

As she slipped along the kennels corridor she heard the girls murmuring in Verla's cell.

She must make a bed for her family, with the skins, keep them warm until the babies grew fur enough to separate them from the mother. On her knees on the floor of her dogbox, the fullness of her pouch swelling below, Yolanda pulled out the pile of skins, and made a little nest. Then, lowering herself so they had no distance to fall, she quietly untied the skins from her body, unbuttoned her tunic and let them fall, squirming, to the furred nest.

The mother rabbit fell, a soft thud. The dark bulbous babies fell, plop slip. They did not squirm. Yolanda waited. They were all asleep.

She scooped them together, the fat little wrigglers that did not wriggle.

No no no.

Pushed the babies to their mother's belly. *Come on, little ones*. She bent her face to the nest, breathed whispering life to them. Wake up, wake up.

IN VERLA'S dogbox they offer up their finds. She sits cross-legged on her bed, sorting through the offerings from their foraging out in the wet paddocks and the mouldy laundry and under the tanks and buildings. Offerings of rag and straw and strings and cloth, dumped on Verla's bed. The girls lean in with their arms folded, drawn to Verla's vision despite themselves. The wind is up again, rain clattering onto the tin roof. They are waiting for Barbs. Yolanda is still out in the fields, gone, she won't help them, but Verla will go into her cell and get a skin or two.

Then come footsteps, Barbs's thundering run, along the corridor. The door is flung back and she bursts in, breathless. 'I found this,' she says, tossing a filthy plastic shopping bag to the bed.

Verla rustles the wet, crumpled bag. Silted with mud, wrenched from some burial ground or rubbish tip.

Barbs breaks into a sob. 'It's our *hair*.'

What! They gather round. Where did she get it? Is she sure?

Barbs wipes her face with her sleeve and rips the bag from Verla, pulls out clumps and plaits and ponytails. The girls snatch and grab at them, recognising their own in the tangled mess of hair, crying out like mother seals for their babies. They are all sobbing now.

Verla searches for her own as the hands rummage and scrabble, finds the curling red fronds. It is astonishing, that this richness might once have belonged to her; even as she holds it to herself she cannot fathom it. Izzy clutches her thick blonde ponytail to herself and strokes it. 'You're not having this, it's mine.' The others repeat her words: they're keeping their hair. Verla draws out a thick, glossy black swatch from the bag and runs it through her hands like velvet rope. She is returned, like a plunge into a cold pool, to the morning she came to consciousness in that room, Yolanda stumbling in, that frightening girl with the waist-length hair. She suddenly wants to cry too, not for her hair but for Yolanda, gone mad with rabbit filth and guts. She cries for the ordinary girl Yolanda once was, who will never return.

She looks into the bag and sees the remaining mess of offcuts of her own red hair, and Hetty's brown furze. And then she looks around herself: crouched on a soiled bed in a room no bigger than a doghouse, surrounded by girls squatting on their haunches, sobbing and combing their fingers through the dead bouquets of their long-lost hair.

They have at last, quite thoroughly, been driven insane. Verla sits, floating on her nest above the circlet of mad girls, and is visited by the paintings in Paris. Madhouses, and mad deeds. The hospital garden at Arles. The hospital at St Remy. This is no hospital, but he made something of his madness.

• • •

When she enters Yolanda's box Verla is startled to find her there on the floor. Hetty's rotting boots lie beside her on the boards.

'I need you to help me make the doll,' Verla says softly. 'I'm using our hair. Barbs found it.'

She holds up Yolanda's length of hair and her own curling tails, one in each hand. Yolanda's eyes are red-rimmed, her face smeared with snot. She looks blankly at the handful of her hair, and takes it from Verla for a moment. The foreign shampoo scent makes her draw back from it. She returns it to Verla. It no longer has anything to do with her.

Only when Verla has taken up a skin from the pile in the corner does she see the little heap of furry bodies in the cradled apron of Yolanda's lap. Yolanda meets her gaze then, and the tears come pouring down.

• • •

Yolanda and Verla worked on the doll all night, in musty candle-light, in silence. Now and then they moved to follow the patch of moonlight on the floor. Through these dark hours the doll became a compulsion, their only purpose. Passing shreds and rags of cloth and rabbit leather back and forth, each following the other's work with the needle or with string. The body was Yolanda's old pillow—she had long ago abandoned it for her piled skins—roughly tied off in places to make breasts, thighs.

It filled them each with something deep, slow-burning, some determination they did not understand, but slowly the doll's misshapen, ugly body grew out of the shames and degradations of their own. One set of hands took over when the other's grew sore from forcing the needle through the fine leather, the sacking and kapok.

• • •

In Verla's hands the pillow torso, stained with tears and sweat, takes shape. She works it in silence, first with delicate stitches of grass, embroidering. *Scented herbage of my breast*, he read to her. *Loveroot, silkthread, crotch and vine*, his finger circled her nipples, moved everywhere. She takes another strand of grass, makes three stitches, it breaks. She takes a length of greyed and bloody gut sinew, her stitches growing finer and more beautiful (*tomb-leaves, body-leaves*), circling and circling with the needle and rabbit gut, and the breasts are worked and worked until finally the headless torso is finished. The breasts are spirals of longing, of lust. The charcoal nipples stick out in urgent pellets, whorled with blood-red stitches. Verla is frightened by this force, her desire. She pushes it from her and climbs up onto Yolanda's bed, lies there with her face turned to the wall.

• • •

Yolanda took up the body then, began at another scarred place, between its thighs. Digging, stabbing, forcing. The doll's dirty pillow flesh yielding beneath her fingers as she pushed and thrust with the needle, crying, working and working at a dark little pocket between its legs, pushing and hollowing, carving out and pushing in.

They had whispered things to her while they used her body. Some made sounds, some grunted, some called her dreadful things, but worst were the ones who used sweet words, horrible sugary epithets, as they rummaged and jerked in her, Yolanda, shapeless and formless and wordless in the dark. Their brothers watching. She did not move, she did not cry out, she would be blamed. She dug her way deep into the long dark corridor, this silent burrow inside herself. Did they know, as they emptied themselves into the rubbish tip of her, about the tunnel in her, was this what they were trying to reach? She held the doll, there in the gloom, Verla asleep on the bed above her. The doll headless, but the body finished. Yolanda saw she had made a womb-burrow inside the doll, just large enough for a tiny rabbit kit. It was not finished.

• • •

Verla wakes from this fitful sleep, the moonlight coming pale and bright through Yolanda's window. Soon it will be morning and Hetty must have her doll, it must be ready. Below her on the floor she sees Yolanda still crouched over the body, her head bent to the task. Verla sits up against the wall, takes up the head from the blankets. Yolanda, still labouring, does not seem to hear her. Verla cradles the blank ball of the head firmly in the crook of her elbow and begins to work again, puncturing the leather scalp to stitch in the first hanks of hair.

In a little while she pauses and looks down to the floor, watching Yolanda finally unbend from the doll body in her lap. She stretches slowly, then reaches behind her, fossicking under the bed. She does not know Verla is awake and watching as she draws out a tiny dead rabbit kit from beneath the bed, cupped in her hand. She doesn't know that Verla is her witness as into the shadowed pockety hole of the doll her fingers push the lifeless, hairless little grey body with a fistful of straw. Yolanda is whispering to herself, some prayer or tender curse or incantation, as she thumbs the creature in, and carefully sews up the hole.

Once it is done, Yolanda lies down on the skins and falls into a deep sleep with the doll's headless, laden body in her arms against her breast, while above her Verla keeps on working at the head.

Sometime in the night there is a noise outside, a tufted ripping.

Thank you, she whispers, as just outside her white horse softly wrenches grass and chews.

• • •

At last the dawn sky lightened outside Yolanda's louvred window.

They got to their knees and crawled away from this doll they had made, and slumped back against the walls. It sat, stiff-backed, among the skins on the floor. Its new dark plaits stuck out, crazed, from its head, each plait strand different: one made of Yolanda's liquorice hair, the second of Verla's woolly red curls, and the third was made of lengths of the last dry ponytail they had found in the bag—Hetty's own hair.

Only now did the two girls look at each other's faces in wonder at what they had made. A totem, it could be, or a ghost. It could be a warrior, voodoo doll, goddess, corpse.

IN THE morning the doll sat, legs sticking out before it, on the veranda boards. From behind the scullery flyscreen door Verla and Yolanda watched Hetty approaching it, suspicious.

It was the size of a large toddler. Its head was a swollen rabbit-leather ball, made of uneven crescents sewn together in difficult lumpy stitches with rabbit gut. Its legs and arms were socks stuffed with the dry grasses from the paddocks. Its body wore scars made with stitches; it appeared somehow tortured, or burnt. The charred-looking nipples made of black rabbit-gut whorls; the distended vulva torn, then savagely repaired. Hetty was hunched above it, peering down, appalled. But she was beginning to recognise what Verla and Yolanda knew, what all the girls would know: that these were battle scars. Something in this embroidered war paint compelled.

Hetty lifted the doll by one stiff rustling arm, and then screamed and dropped it. She had recognised her own hair, plaited in with Verla's locks and Yolanda's thick black strands. She crouched beside it now, silent, staring at it, taking in its voodoo portent, its power.

Boncer was there now too, gawping. He had followed Hetty out onto the cold veranda and stood in his bare feet, stepping from one side to the other, mesmerised by the shocking ugly doll.

Hetty stood and rounded on him. 'Where did they get this thing?!'

He only stared, arms folded, his face shrivelled in marvelling disgust. 'I dunno.'

Something in the doll made him quail, and he turned back to Hetty, filled with fearful lust, with mummy's-boy need. He reached out to touch her breast. But Hetty smacked his hand away. 'Fuck off,' she muttered. He reared back, injured.

'It has no face,' she said, peering down at the doll. But the body sat in a nest of Yolanda's finest rabbit furs and Hetty could not resist crouching again, reaching out to touch. The morning was cold, and the fur was warm.

'Come here, baby girl,' wheedled Boncer, reaching. 'I need you.'

Only then did Hetty look up and see Verla and Yolanda waiting behind the screen door. Boncer stroked Hetty's neck. Hetty stared at them while he did it.

'Come on,' he said, tugging at her dress.

Hetty closed her eyes, sighed.

'Come *on*,' said Boncer testily. His old self returning. He did not have his stick, but his hand feathered the air for it, and Hetty heard it in his voice.

'All right,' she said in a low, resigned voice, fixing her gaze once more on the doll. As Boncer took her arm in his bony grasp she snatched up the doll. And she looked back at Verla and Yolanda, holding it to her chest like a baby or a shield as Boncer led her back up the veranda and into the corridor, away to his room.

• • •

Late that afternoon they sat at the refectory table, waiting for the stew. It was Izzy and Barbs's turn in the kitchen, so it would be edible at least. It was Barbs who had declared that eating only rabbit would kill them—Stephen Fry said it on *QI*, so it was true—and so sent the girls all foraging for weeds each day. She boiled up the piles of stalks and leaves in her stockpot with salt, testing and tasting the green muck. Three different weeds turned out to be edible—or at least could be taken without spitting them out for bitterness—but the prize, the most desirable, was the long, scalloped dandelion leaf. For weeks now whenever a dandelion plant—or, even better, a patch—was found, a little shout of triumph could be heard across the paddocks.

Verla's mushroom experiments were still a secret. Only Yolanda could know, lest the carelessness of the other girls alert Boncer. Verla trailed Yolanda when she went stalking her traps in the dawn, collecting and concealing the fresh mushrooms in her clothes until she could hide them in the meat locker.

Now Yolanda slumped at the table and dozed, her head on her arms. Across the table Verla swayed in her chair, hardly able to keep her own eyes open. The others watched them, knowing they had been up all night doing something, but they had not yet seen Hetty's doll. They still purred and whispered excitedly about their hair, the ponytails they had taken to their beds, nuzzling them, winding them between their fingers, tucking them beneath their pillows, into their nightdresses. They had been given new life, new hope, from these tendrils of their girl selves. If the hair was found, other parts of themselves might be recoverable too.

Boncer's and Hetty's places at the table were empty, Nancy's and Teddy's too. Teddy had slouched around after Nancy since she learned about Hetty and Boncer. It seemed Nancy would be his sole responsibility now; he spent the day following in her wavering footsteps, trying to stop her cutting herself or swallowing pills. For an hour he tried to teach her some yoga poses, but she only slumped, moaning, on the boards beside him.

Teddy came in now. A scrawny, clumsily made noose hung from his pocket.

She couldn't really mean it, the girls said, or she would have gone to the fence.

A sweet, cloying smell mingled with rabbit came from the kitchen. They salivated with hunger. Days ago Izzy had found a carton of Home Selection Apricot Chicken powder sachets in the last box in the storeroom. The bright orange gloop made a pleasing change. In the restful dark of her folded arms Yolanda thought again of her grandmother, who used to make apricot chicken, but the real stuff: apricots in syrup from a can, and French onion soup mix. Yolanda's own mother would roll her eyes, but Yolanda and Darren loved it. But that was chicken, actual chicken.

She sat up when the door was flung open and Boncer came in, carrying an extra chair. He set it down between his and

Hetty's places. He pulled it out. The girls slowly straightened, waiting.

Hetty entered. The girls gasped, for in her arms she carried the doll. Their faces swung to Verla and Yolanda, who had made this terrible thing, then back again to Hetty, who stood, allowing herself to be inspected.

She looked exhausted, but in her tired eyes was a kind of violence, and power. The doll no longer disgusted her; she seemed to enjoy the air shivering when the girls saw it, clutched to her body. She approached the table, shifting the doll to her hip, as if she carried a real infant, moving with a queenly air. Some new nobility had settled on Hetty in the face of this thing, this appalling royal baby. She arranged the doll in the extra chair, flouncing out its rabbit-skin rugs, and then sat, dignified, beside it. Boncer stood behind and pushed both chairs in.

In the dim light of the ref the doll took its place at the table.

Izzy came in, carrying dishes of steaming orange slop. She saw the doll and jolted, let out a cry. Backed away from it, put down the two plates and fled again to the kitchen. When she came back, recovered, she was followed by Barbs, who had been warned, who stared but remained composed. They moved silently around the table, setting down plates. When Barbs got to Hetty she hesitated, held the plate aloft.

'Does . . . ?' Nodding at the terrible baby.

'Don't be stupid,' snapped Hetty. 'It's a doll.'

They sat and set to eating, noisily but without speaking, watched by Hetty's faceless rabbit-leather doll.

Later she would christen it Ransom, but now it was just the doll. The ten girls sucked on rabbit bones beneath its eyeless gaze.

part three:
WINTER

YOLANDA PADDED out of the dogboxes and past the house, moving silently in the dawn light. She had stuck Hetty's flapping boot sole together with mashed rabbit guts, and then wound a long scrap of the skin around to bind it while the gluey mess of it set. She left it for a day and a night until the glue hardened, but in that day discovered the warmth of the rabbit fur. So with the next skin she wound a boot glove for her other foot. At first she rolled on the soles; it was like walking on knobbled grass. But her ankles grew accustomed, she found a new walk, and she soon felt naked without them.

Breathing out mist with each exhalation, she crossed the flat. The mornings were very cold now when she rose in the dark and slipped her feet into the rabbit-skin boots, pulled the stiff, buckling cloak of skins about her, fastened it round with the belt, weighed down by the traps. Over the months she had pushed a knife through the skins to make buttonholes, then tied them with rags. On her calloused hands she wore great fur mitts, gauntlets glued with gizzards and stitched with gut.

The sun was still hidden but a faint pink tidemark was rising with the dawn behind the ridge. On she walked, up the side of the dry basin. After a time she stopped to shift the traps on her belt. She looked back across the plain. She had climbed the hill in the gloom but now the sky was lightening she could see that the grass was pinwheeled with small frosted cobwebs: handspans of silver gauze suspended between grass-blades. Hundreds, perhaps a thousand of them, all across the paddock below her. She stood as the sky glowed, and more and more cobweb stars became visible. A Milky Way across the flat.

She shivered and pushed on up the side, the traps chinking against her. The skins kept her body and hands and feet warm but her face was icy. The sun would soon be up; she would lift her face to its pale warmth.

The days had settled into an easier rhythm since Hetty had delivered herself to Boncer and he spent his time sniffing and wheedling after her, ignoring the rest.

Verla had her mushroom project, collecting and sorting and hiding. Rhiannon tramped off to the ute skeleton every day, driving herself to an imaginary coast. Leandra chopped kindling and fed the stove, playing house with Barbs, who carried the stockpot around, playing Little House on the Prairie with an infant on her hip. Hetty had given up her prayers now she had the doll to play with. Joy and Izzy and Lydia had their tweezers and makeovers and mantras (*the skin is the body's largest organ*, Lydia preached to Joy and Izzy, who nodded reverently, picking through each other's hair for nits). Maitlynd squatted by the tank feeding her fat lurking frog, or patrolled the windowsills, collecting moths.

It could not be said, even if Yolanda still used her voice, but increasingly she found things beautiful out here in the paddocks. This pink sky, these starry cobwebs. At night she dreamed herself with claws, digging a burrow. Tunnelling out under the fence, into the teeming bush. Not returning to her old life, never back there, but inwards, downwards, running on all fours, smelling the grass and the earth as familiar as her own body. She dreamed of an animal freedom.

Verla had her private dreams too, Yolanda knew. Not just her poisoning-Boncer plot (a fantasy, but who was Yolanda to puncture it?), but though Verla no longer mentioned it, Yolanda knew she still scanned the hillsides for her imaginary white horse, still believed it to come nibbling round the dogboxes at night.

Three white cockatoos screeched overhead, their wings lit pink by the sunrise. She squatted over the first trap—empty, not for the first time here, she would need to move it. A cloud moved across the sun, making her shiver again. There was a noise: a great sigh coming from the ridge. It was not a cloud that made her stand and stare as a vast orange curve appeared, lipping the black trees.

It was a balloon. A hot-air balloon. An enormous, pleated bulb in the clear brightening sky. Frosty breath plumed out from her lips. No sound came from her. The balloon rose higher. It was just high enough to skim the treetops. It swept, scooped across the air towards her, above her. It was like a planet from another universe, almost touching hers and moving fast, and soon it would be gone.

She looked back down the bank of the hill towards the house, the outbuildings. No figures moved, no smoke rose, nothing was visible in the paddocks or around the dogboxes. Verla was not to be seen. There was no-one but Yolanda to take part in this visitation, this drifting dream. Her feet were rooted to the earth. A blast of air roared again, and the approaching planet lifted a little in the sky. Its immense shadow swept along, seizing Yolanda's heart.

There were people. Two, three, maybe five, looking down from their basket beneath the great canopy, swimming through the sky towards her. She could hear their voices. Yolanda's fingers went to her belt, unbuckled it, dropped the traps. She began to run. She would scream, *Help us*. She ran, stumbling from looking up. Soon it would overtake her. *Please*, she called, but her voice was a low croak. Yet two faces peered down, saw her. She ran, began to wave. She could hear the people, their voices clear in the crisp air. They called to the others, and then all five appeared at one side of the basket, leaning over, pointing down at her. The balloon drifted, bounced in the air.

Yolanda ran, chasing and scrambling across the rough earth. She would cry out, *We are prisoners. Get help.* She panted, running and running to keep up. But no words came, only a whimper. The people watched her, waving, their arms swinging lazily, pendulums against the sky.

'Hello!' they called down. 'Beautiful morning!' There were delighted whoops as the balloon sank lower and then rose again, skidding across the valley. They cheered Yolanda as she chased. She stumbled but would not stop running. *Help us*, she tried to cry out. Could they hear her panting breath? Surely they must see, must hear her. The balloon began to lift higher and higher. She bellowed then: a noise, a wounded sound, not human. They cheered. Yolanda sprinted, roaring up at them, waving her rabbit-mittened hands in the air. The balloon was swept up then in a rush, and hoots of surprise and laughter came down. One of the people leaned over the edge, calling, 'Byee!' And there was a pop and they were drinking champagne.

Yolanda roared her trapped-animal's cry.

'Bye-bye,' they called, laughing and waving and clinking their glasses. The balloon lifted higher and drifted off across the scoured pink sky. It seemed to slow down and darken as it rose, up and up, and the blue sky was dotted now with pure white scuffs of cloud, and the balloon slowly shrank so that it was soon just a dark pinhole in the endless sky. Yolanda stood watching that other world that had come so close, spinning away.

'HOW STUPID do you think I am?' Boncer sneers across the table.

How fucking stupid? He raises his stick and Verla ducks, covering her ears and head.

Nobody else moves. The girls sit very still, staring at the table surface. Each inspecting the small patch of laminate before her, very intently and closely, as if it is an intricate map of a tiny country only she can visit, if she makes herself go still enough and small enough, while she waits for the table to jump and the bowls to shatter with a stroke of Boncer's familiar rage.

The plates are filled with rabbit stew, but for the first time there is also a little heap of sliced mushrooms on each one. It is this that has him on his feet.

These last weeks he has been so altered, it has been like a holiday. But this evening, because of Verla, his old savagery has returned. She, with her mushrooms, has brought the old Boncer back and she feels like heat the girls' anger coming at her. Even Hetty shrivels into her old furtive self, clutching the doll to her chest, watching Boncer sidelong, ready to duck from his raised stick if it falls in her direction. Nancy and Teddy are motionless, alert, at the end of the table.

But Boncer does not hit anyone. He sees Hetty's chin tucked under, resting on the doll's head, and the lover's tenderness laps over him again. He puts a hand out to Hetty, stroking her head like a puppy's. She is always beside him now, Ransom clasped to her or slung across her body like a grubby satchel, limp sock-arm pinned to dingy foot, as Hetty walks. At mealtimes, it is either sat stiffly in her lap, so she has to reach around it to eat, or has its own chair drawn up. Sometimes Hetty jounces it in her arms like a real baby.

Boncer gives Hetty an apologetic glance, and Verla sees Hetty remembering her new role, her triumphs and how to inhabit them. Her queenly bearing returns with a little nod to Boncer, and a nasty grin at Verla. She sits back in her chair, patting Ransom's grass-stuffed back soothingly. It makes a thackety sound.

To Verla, Boncer says, 'You eat it, you murderous slut.'

He spins his plate across the table to Verla so fast she has to put out a hand to stop it, and the rabbit gravy slops against her

242

skin, hot. She sucks a splash from her wrist. Then she looks him in the eye and fingers up a slice of mushroom into her mouth, chews it once, swallows. It is hard not to close her eyes at the pleasure of it. Boncer is hungry, watching her. She runs her tongue around her teeth, swallows again. Will she risk raising an eyebrow at him? No, she will not, the stick still in his hand.

'You want me to eat more?' she says quietly, wiping a drip of mushroom gravy from her chin.

He's yearning for the taste, she can see it in his face, but he says, 'All of it. Off all the plates.'

Then she does risk a smile, reaches for her fork. One by one the girls push their plates across to her, and she eats the mushrooms from each one. She chews and swallows, the squeaky portobellos cooked in rabbit juice, and the smell of it is unbearably good. The girls hunch with their hands in their armpits, sucking their teeth with hunger.

Yolanda watches her with the rest.

Another plate comes her way; she picks off the mushrooms and again swallows them. Pushes the plate back, takes the next, eats from it, wipes up the juices with her finger and licks it. Boncer stares bitterly, one arm draped around Hetty's neck. They all wait. Then, when she has finished all the mushrooms and the plates of rabbit meat are in front of the girls again, they

243

are allowed to eat. They lean in, gobbling like dogs. But Boncer won't touch his. He watches Verla, all malevolence. He turns and takes a good long look at Yolanda bolting down the meat, her face near her plate, her black hair a mass of dirty tails. Boncer looks hungry, but not for food. Still staring at Yolanda, he leans and kisses Hetty violently, like a bite, on the neck. Hetty jerks sideways, startled, but she is accustomed now to these incursions on her body. She closes her eyes and regains her balance, as a mother sheep withstands a lamb's butting, and keeps eating.

Verla sits trying to will herself warm. She is so cold, she can't remember what it is like not to be cold, this clammy air on your skin. Every part of her, even beneath the blankets at night, is damp and cold. Outside, the rain beats down, as it has done all day and all the night before. The ceaseless thrum of it will accompany Verla's sleep, never deep, her legs drawn up, searching all through the night for warmth.

And now Boncer knows her plan. She rubs her hands between her knees, curls and uncurls her toes inside the damp rotting leather of her boots. Across the table Yolanda hunkers, her plate in both hands, licking it clean. Oblivious to the cold.

A funky warm stink rises off her skins.

• • •

That night it is so cold that Verla gets up from her bed, leaving her thin ratty blanket. She slowly slides her bolt across and lets herself out of her box, pads down the corridor to Yolanda's. She knocks softly on the door, and whispers, 'It's me.'

She hears the squeak of iron bedsprings, and then, tall and naked in the icy moonlight, Yolanda stands at the open door to receive her. She draws her in, closes and bolts the door behind Verla as she clambers into Yolanda's furry nest. And in a moment they are curled together, Verla's knees drawn up beneath her nightdress, soft with the months of grime and wear, the warmth of her friend's body curved around her back. It is so long since she felt the pulse of another human heart. But it is an animal's heart that beats in Yolanda now.

Verla dreams that a lamb's head is brought to her, and she must wear it. She pulls it on, her own head squishing up inside the wet opening of the lambskin neck, tugging until its narrow skull is forced down, hard, over hers. The neck opening, dripping, reaches to her shoulders. Its sodden woollen fronds cold against her bare neck. Then she must don the body of the lamb, the skin, her body replacing its own, its entrails spilling out like bathwater. She must occupy the lamb's body. She looks out of its blood-rimmed eyes at a cold, pink-stained world.

• • •

Back in the meat locker she tries again, with a new kind of mushroom. It must be hallucinogenic, for each nibble takes her away. Her father, what would he be doing now? He will miss her, speechlessly, and nobody will know.

This briny bulb, pressed to her nose, is the smell of seaweed wrapped around her ankle at the little sandy beach beneath the jetty. She lets the vision take hold of her in the damp dark room.

There were days she would wheel him down to the jetty and park him there while she smoked, and then unwrap the fish-and-chip paper and feed each sliver into his grinning, vulnerable mouth. Salt crystals on his white tongue and his cracked lips, his leaning yellow teeth. His ghost's hand caressing the air with his gentle, tender mania.

She never knew it then, only puzzled over her mother's frozen immobility and how it mirrored his, as if his brain insult fired in her hemispheres too, before she left again for East Timor and almost never came back. But she knows now, inhaling her damaged baby-brained father with the mushroom's spores, that only the young could do these things for the old. Now she has been aged by her months here, she understands that only a girl with a blithe enjoyment of her own living flesh, only the young with a peach-fat, glossy mind could joyously thread hot potato chips into the mouth of her witless old father. Back then she could not conceive of waste or decay. She could offer her pitiless attention because his decay had nothing to do with her living.

In this way she and her father had wordless conversations through the long afternoons, about many things. After she had begun with Andrew, and it had got complicated, she found it soothing to wheel her father down there and sit by him, his weathervane hand coasting the air, watching the pelicans and the gulls sink and lift in the dirty water. Sometimes she would reach up to adjust his neck scarf, and he would close his eyes in approval, and murmur his only remaining word, *bloody*, but she knew he meant it as gratitude.

The whole spring and summer of Andrew she would do this, arrive in the hallway and snap the folding wheelchair open, saying, 'Come on, Dad,' and smile over his shoulder at the prim-lipped nurse. Verla put her arms around him to lift and guide him in their shuffling little corpse's rhumba to the chair, then let him drop—*hughh*—into it. Then she tidied his limbs, packaged him up and slung the scarf around him, ignored the nurse about therapy and time for this or that.

Verla would charge him down the ramp, veering too fast and dangerous, jerkily halt for the turn around the corner (sometimes seeing his frightened hands grip the armrests), but once out on the street they would calm down, she would wheel him slower and feel him relax into the chair. And she would silently tell him everything as they wheeled and strolled, eased by his warm dumb animal presence, and the fact that he loved her effortlessly, the fact that he was her father.

In the gloom of the meat locker, Verla holds the brittle mushroom and mashes it to her mouth and nose and crumbles it, softly mourning the comfort of her father, sorry for his loneliness and his wondering why she hasn't come to see him.

After a time she brushes the crumbs of the mushroom away. Her father may be dead or alive, stuck in his chair in the respite day centre, or perhaps somehow liberated, driven off the end of the jetty and drowned. She sends him out a prayer: *I am still your daughter.*

She gets to work, documenting this one. Dry, briny, a piece of brown coral, one and a half thumbs high, three fingers broad. So far—that was, within seventy-two minutes—flooding memories, hallucinations maybe, but no poison.

She makes a little hoop of bark for it and puts it in the ice chest to dry.

• • •

When she finds the death cap it is so clearly, so obviously itself that she almost laughs out loud. How could she have mistaken those others? She knows it instantly, even from here, yards away. Even before she kneels at it in the wet grass, something in her starts up at the sight of it, the burnished glisten of its hooded cap. Up close, she sees the butting, insistent head, the thick white stalk, the useless flared skirt beneath the cap. And when she inspects it with a stick, the gills. Pure white.

Verla lies on her belly in the wet grass, holding off picking it, admiring it, wondering at it, in love. Then she turns onto her back, staring up at the sky. A pleat of blue has opened up in the clouds. It is a long, fresh valley, waiting for her.

• • •

When Hetty totters into the ref the next day, the bloody lamb's head of Verla's dream returns to her. The plates of her own skull bones begin cracking inwards as the beast's suedey skull is forced down over hers, her vision laced with blue-veined membranes. It must be the dream, this net of blood across her vision, or why else does Hetty seem to be wearing Verla's own red zippered jacket?

Now a scuffle across the room, a bellow, chairs knocked sideways and down. Yolanda has her hands at Hetty's throat,

Lydia screams, *You fucking slag*, they are all tearing and clawing at her, even under Boncer's flashing flailing stick. It strikes bone, breaks skin, they fall away gasping and roaring. Teddy is there, dragging Yolanda off. Hetty hides behind Boncer, winded and sobbing, pressing her flat hand to what must be Yolanda's little reindeer necklace from Darren at her throat.

The room is panting and screaming. Yolanda no longer bellows, knocked to the floor with blood down her neck in a bright twirling necklace of her own, but mutters, her breath heaving, staring bright and vicious at Hetty, *You are gone, you are gone, you are gone.*

Teddy has Barbs's upper arm gripped; she struggles and spits at the *treacherous bitch*, and Teddy hisses at Boncer, 'Why'dja even bring her in here, you fucking idiot?'

Boncer's voice has a calm new ferocity and he is telling the truth when he says, 'Any of you touch her again and I will kill you.' And now they see that it is not his stick he has been hitting them with but a long black pole, and he is pointing it at them. It weaves through the air, his black and silver wand. They stare, for what is it? Some kind of mop, some pruning shears, hedge trimmers, but there at the end, a pistol handle.

'That's my spear gun!' Teddy roars.

Boncer swipes the air with the silver point of it, aimed at Teddy, along with his smile. The spear, its savage hooks, suddenly visible. 'That's right. Now siddown and eat your fucking dinner.'

They sit. Teddy breathing hard, Nancy with her blank, hollow eyes shuffling closer to Teddy on the bench. Boncer's sparkling violence, their own shock at what they have seen, commands them all. The girls sit and bleed, scrape their bowls in silence, the swallow of a sob now and then, grief pouring from the eyes of every girl for what Hetty has done.

For now they are all hostage to this ugly little family: Hetty in their stolen clothes, Boncer with his fearsome spear gun, and Ransom, their mouldering baby, splay-legged on the chair between them.

Hetty preens by Boncer's side so they can thoroughly take her in. Beneath Verla's red canvas jacket she wears Lydia's black T-shirt with its giant orange spots; lower, her dirty thighs come out of Joy's short shorts, pale denim, only just covering her arse. She wears Yolanda's little gold reindeer around her neck. And on her feet, yes, Hetty wears Izzy's new Chloé ankle boots, the ones Izzy has cried and cried over ever since they arrived. Black suede, six-inch heels. Hetty tilts one ankle, holds on to Boncer and then the chair in front of her. She flicks her dirty hair over her shoulder, and then clambers into the chair, her thick waist pushing against Verla's jacket, the stitching stretching, and draws a bowl towards herself.

It is the colours of the clothes that so shock, that declare anew how degraded they have become. They cannot take their eyes off the red, the orange spots. It is pure, mesmerising, saturated colour. They marvel at it, in disbelief that they once took no notice of such shocking bludgeons, this startling beauty surrounding them, carried on their own bodies. They see themselves, each other, afresh. Filthy, grey-toothed, pock-skinned, lice-ridden. Their tunics colourless, torn, frayed and stinking. Their rotting brown boots. And how their skin has thickened with the cold and the wind and the sun, their lips blistered, their cheeks rasped. Even Hetty's thighs are gooseflesh, though the rest of her body is warm beneath the red canvas and the pristine boots.

Verla knows the warmth and softness of that mourned jacket, feels her old life pulsing from somewhere inside it, held in by the snug toughness of the zipper sliding up over her breasts. She closes her eyes and swallows the strings of rabbit flesh, and returns to her dream. She pulls the head down, draws close the lambskin, its shreds of fat and blood and tissue clinging. This dreamed body she will occupy until Boncer is dead, and

Hetty too, and then she will lift that red jacket away, as lightly as the petal of a poppy, and leave her lying naked to be picked over by the birds.

• • •

Ransom has begun to stink. The rank smell follows Hetty wherever she goes, but she will not put down the doll nor leave it outside. Only Yolanda and Verla know about the little corpse sewn inside. But they say nothing, even to each other, as with the others they cover their noses and mouths whenever Hetty totters near them, already scuffing Izzy's boots. Let Hetty carry her decaying baby. Let her rot with it.

• • •

They line up along the table each evening, each evening the same plates are brought in, the same thing happens. Boncer eyes them while they eat the mushrooms and rabbit and weeds. Even Hetty eats it. She sits in her stolen clothes, the stinking doll beside her on a chair. Boncer is both king and royal guard, his spear gun vertical beside them, held in his fist as tightly as a beefeater's bayonet.

Teddy is afraid of Boncer now. One afternoon he tried to talk him into unloading the spear gun shaft, told him how a single bump might set it off, kill Hetty by accident, even Boncer himself. Boncer eyed him, looked at the taut rubber band holding the shaft in place. But then he said, 'Shut up, faggot,' and pointed the gun at Teddy to make him run. So Teddy scrambled along the veranda with his backpack—a bright blue wetsuit arm flapped from its opened top and he carried orange flippers dangling from one hand—and moved into Nancy's sick bay for good.

Here at the table Boncer watches Hetty eat. He has tried to stop her eating the mushrooms but she is too greedy. She gobbles them down as he inspects her, eyes watering with fear, watching her for signs of poison.

Like the others Verla eats the food without tasting, her eyes on the chipped greying bowl. H A R D I N G S spelled out around the rim. How strange that they once feared or expected Hardings, that mythical beast. They might as well have hoped for unicorns or dragons.

Suddenly Boncer's hand shoots out and claws Yolanda's plate towards him, leaving her fork in mid-air. 'I'll have this one,' he says, and scoffs the plateful, his face close to the dish. He closes his eyes, just once, at the taste, finally, of the mushroom.

Each night after that he takes a plate from a different girl.

THE AIR has lost its sharpness, and the sun is over the ridge now. Winter is receding.

When Verla follows Yolanda like this, at a distance, other things recede too. Her thoughts can come and go with a simple clarity, unburdened by the gruelling marrow of misery lying along her bones in the dogbox, fouling her mind the rest of the time, in the ref, anywhere near Boncer or Hetty or Nancy. Or even Teddy, now at Boncer's mercy too (but there is no pity for him, not from Verla). Out here in the paddocks and up on the ridge, she understands, they are . . . unregarded. Not threatened with sticks or being tied up or leashed or speared. They are not sluts or prisoners. Not even girls, here, but something like seeds, blown by the wind.

She looks up into the frail glimmer of the sun, which lights this ridge as it has done forever. She would like to thank it.

As if the cold morning air freshens her, Yolanda moves swiftly ahead, rapidly moving away from Verla in the furry mittens of her rabbit boots, gliding through the prickling grass and over the tussocky ground.

Today Verla follows easily, her scoping gaze careful, clean across the paddocks as she moves behind Yolanda. She knows now where mushrooms are likely to be found, predicts their small domed forms before she sees them, barely stops as she stoops to pull them from the earth and scoop them into the sling across her chest. Back in the meat locker, hidden in the hollow of the corrugated iron behind a post, are three sticky little death caps swaddled in a small piece of tattered cloth. She has not seen one for several weeks now, but the search is no longer urgent. Now that Boncer has taken to eating from a different girl's plate each night, she has no idea how she will get him poisoned. He watches her bring the mushrooms to the kitchen each day, has searched her meat locker but found nothing.

To be so close to his death but unable to bring it about, is unbearable.

Yolanda turns and begins to labour up the western curve. Verla can hear no breathing from her, she moves without sound, though the walking is steep now and difficult. Verla scrabbles along behind with some effort. The sloping stony path makes balance hard. She no longer pretends she is fit enough to keep up. Eventually, Yolanda will stop and wait for her, looking past her down the long sweep of the hill to where they began their climb as Verla bends to catch her breath, hands on her knees.

Does Yolanda remember that first glazed, terrifying day, marching up here, clipped to the others and Boncer? How long ago that was, like a dream. How altered they are. Now, when Verla tries to remember herself, that long-ago girl struggling to the surface of her sedation that day, she cannot. It is as if she is trying to inhabit some other creature, some impossible existence, like that of a cuttlefish, a worm, a tree. Yolanda is more changed than any of them. Are they friends? Verla considers this, trudging. Perhaps, but in the bodily, speechless way of a man and his dog. Yolanda does not want human friendship, Verla knows. She looks for her up ahead—she has not stopped after all, is striding away up the hillside, not slowing or waiting, a small figure moving steadily, appearing and disappearing again against the land's muted tones in the grey camouflage of her animal skins.

Verla pushes a strand of hair from her forehead and moves off again, sweat at her underarms and her groin.

The sun slowly lifts.

She can hear the fence. Some days she thinks it has stopped—but when they've neared it, they realise it's only that the sound is so familiar to them now it is as the sound of the birds or the ceaseless wind. Some days, like today, when the wind is coming from the right direction, its hum is loud. It will never stop, she knows bitterly; it is as endless as the sky.

Verla has not seen her horse in weeks. At night she gets out of bed and waits for it. Last night she took herself out beneath the moonlight, calling for it in a secret whisper, searching the dark plains and hills and outcrops of the buildings for a glimpse of its pale shifting form, her bare feet cold on the frosty earth, but she did not see it. She knows it is out here, plodding the hills somewhere, its long teeth grasping and wrenching at the grass. Sustaining itself, biding its time. It is another certainty that has come to Verla with the death cap: that the horse and she are bound in some way. That in a sense the horse is her, Verla, in some liberated, ghostly form. And one day—after things are done with Boncer—the horse and she will be united. She cannot say how, or what this will mean, but deep in herself she knows it. It will return, and she will clamber up to lie along its warm breathing body and rest her cheek in its ragged, burr-studded mane. It will carry her out to her rightful life, to the little Whitman book, to Andrew waiting with cries of sorrow and poetry.

She presses on, panting, up the crest. At last she catches up with Yolanda, who has stopped, standing above her, her hands clasped behind her head. Silhouetted against the sky, she is a warrior creature in furs, stinking of rabbit piss and death, muscled like a man. As soon as Verla reaches her, Yolanda turns and forges on. Only one more trap to check. It has the sense of a quest, today. Verla is tiring; she stops looking for mushrooms. She stays close to Yolanda now, just above her on the path, so she is face to face with the bunch of tied rabbits swinging from Yolanda's belt. She watches their heads and staring eyes, their long soft bodies swaying with the motion of Yolanda's stride.

Yolanda grunts as they round a large rock in their path, stopping so suddenly Verla bumps up against her. The furred columns of the rabbit corpses brush against her own body; she rears back, repelled.

Yolanda has stopped because there is no rabbit in the last trap. The earth in the clearing around it has been shovelled, ploughed. The trap's long steel pin is still wedged beneath the great weight of the stone, but its jaws have snared the long, smooth foot of a large grey kangaroo. It is alive. It has been lying awkwardly on its side, but at their approach has shuffled upright. The trapped, bloody foot forces it to lurch and sway, its head dipped. Its little forelegs dangle, useless, at its chest.

Verla stood in the bush with the kangaroos hurtling past her. This happened, she thinks, it wasn't just a fever. She feels it again, the rush of air. The velocity, that animal force. But now this bedraggled creature.

How has this happened? With any of the other traps Yolanda has set, a single jerk from such a large animal would have pulled the pin from the ground. The roo would have to drag the snapped trap with it, but would not be captive like this. But here, something in the angle of the pin beneath the rock has it stuck fast. As it jerks and strains, the pinned chain is yanked taut.

The roo is as tall as the girls. They can smell the animal breath coming at them, dank and afraid.

It stops struggling and stares straight at them. Ears vertical, twitching, quivering. The thick, muscular trunk of its tail presses into the dirt, supporting its great weight. The girls stand, unmoving, not speaking. Vainly, the kangaroo shifts and scuffles again. Then it lowers its head and lengthens its mighty neck, black eyes fixed on them, and lets out three long, hoarse snarls. Its snout fattens, nostrils flared. Panting with effort, it falls to rest back on the great stool of its tail. Little balls of shit lie everywhere about the clearing.

'Have to unclamp the trap,' Yolanda whispers, and takes a tentative step towards the creature.

Verla hisses, 'You can't!' Its claws, even on the delicate forefeet, are long and sharp; the great hind claws are thick, carved blades. To free the trap, Yolanda would have to crouch with those black scalpels beside her face. She lowers herself to a squat, begins shuffling towards it on her haunches. The kangaroo lowers its long head and thrusts towards her, lets out another dry, warning growl: louder than before, higher pitched, a threat. Verla has a vision of the great body launched at Yolanda, her rabbit-skin belly slit open with one kick, the features torn from her face by the little black foreclaws. Yolanda scrambles backwards at its warning growl. She gets to her feet, flushed, shame flooding in after her survival instinct. Verla knows her heart is beating fast.

'What will happen to it?' asks Verla. In some hidden part of her a seed husk is cracking, peeling open. To do with this maimed kangaroo, to do with her night-stepping horse. A fear has been forming inside her, she sees now, since the horse went missing. And it swells in her, carrying with it a low thrum, like the hum of the fence. She wants to turn and run back down the stony ridge. She wants never to have seen this omen. Verla's pallid, beautiful moon horse sick somewhere, caught like this.

The question needs no answer but Yolanda says it anyway. Perhaps to herself. 'It'll die.'

They stand apart, watching the kangaroo, its impotent weaving and panting. It is unbearable. They cannot leave it like this.

'We're frightening it,' whispers Verla, grasping Yolanda's arm to pull her behind the boulder, out of sight of the animal. If it could rest, perhaps it might heal, free itself.

Yolanda leans against the stone, pinching her lip. Her rabbit-skirts trailing from her belt. She is of the earth now, Verla thinks. She has animal comprehension, will find a way. She squats in the shadow of the rock, sits on the damp earth.

'We have to get it water,' Verla says.

Yolanda shakes her head. 'Kinder to hit it on the head.' She begins scanning the grass for a stone.

'No!'

That cold, hunter's gaze turning on her. 'What's the matter?'

If they bring it water and food—Verla pushes a thumb over and over across her palm, she knows she is begging—it might grow strong enough to dislodge the pin from beneath the rock. (Her horse, somewhere, panting, captive.) It mustn't die.

Yolanda snorts. 'Then what? It drags the trap around, dies more slowly, in agony, of infection?'

But she peers around the rock, and Verla can tell that even the hunter in her is moved by the roo's exhausted, mournful face, its terrible aloneness. She recognises it. The animal is separated from all of life, yet in anguish still blindly lives. It is her trap that has done this.

When she turns back, Verla sees her face and knows they will return with food and water.

They creep around the rock to take one last look at the struggling creature. It pants at them again, and they breathe it in. Before they turn to go, Verla unwinds her mushroom cloth, tosses the pieces to the ground near the roo. Yolanda shakes her head at this foolishness.

'It might take them,' Verla says, but the roo only shuffles again, frightened by the rolling things, and then flops down again, watching them with its helpless, glittering gaze.

They walk and do not speak. They will tell nobody what they have seen. They think of Boncer's spear gun, his braying laugh. They hold their own secrets to themselves as they walk: of burrowing claws, of sorrow, of pale slow-moving shapes in the moonlit night.

• • •

The next day the kangaroo did not stir as they made their way through the grass around the rock. They sat in the shadow of the stone, watching it. The flies were worse over its foot, now swollen around the metal of the trap. Now and then the animal let out a low grunt, a suffering sound. It was too near death to have touched the water bowl or the grass they had pushed towards it with a stick yesterday. They could see the black blowflies bubbled along the jaws of the trap, busy at the jammy blackened wound. The kangaroo's head now lay in the dust. It gazed down at the foot with clouded disinterest. A few more small flies slowly orbited its head. Its ears flicked occasionally, ineffectively, to ward them off. Its mouth was open, panting softly.

'We can't do anything for him,' said Yolanda, stepping out from under the curve of the rock. Except what she could do with the stone in her hand. There was something human about the roo's fallen shape, the back arched, the good leg drawn up to its belly where the little hands were crossed. The thick trunk of the tail stretched out behind it, limp and useless now. The testicles lay exposed in their sac on the flat yellow ground.

264

When Yolanda sat down cross-legged in the dirt beside it, the kangaroo no longer started or lurched. Verla stared from alongside the rock, her hands jammed into her armpits. Her gaze was on the free foot and the forefeet claws, but she looked vacant, outside herself and this place. Yolanda shuffled nearer to the animal, lifted its long, elegant face into her lap. It was too weak for anything but a small, unresisting shudder. Yolanda took the jar and tried to tip water into its mouth, but it could not swallow. The water soaked its fur and Yolanda's tunic. She saw something coming from its nose. She had to hold her breath to stop from inhaling in its rank smell, lifted her head to the side and gulped air now and then. She looked across at Verla, the dying animal in her lap.

There was no point in trying to remove the trap now, and there would be no need to use the stone, for it would very soon be dead. The kangaroo's belly rose and fell with rapid, shallow breaths.

• • •

In Rome, Verla saw the marble mother cradle her gleaming dead son. Andrew explained how miraculously out of proportion was the Pietà, in order that Mary's arms could hold the whole man; he went on about stone and sculptor, but in that bustling domed space Verla felt there was only herself and the woman. She understood her, as if those were Verla's own fingers pressing against slack lifeless flesh. The limp and dreadful shoulder hanging, the mother's strong fingers pressing. And now here Yolanda sits, her own pietà in the dirty grass beneath a bright cold sky, crooning and snuffling, murmuring into the dusty fur, cradling and rocking.

Verla knows something terrible has happened to her moonlight horse.

The roo's shuddering noises, those testicles on the grass, her father in a hospital gown being helped to the toilet by her mother. Verla, eleven, watching the suddenly-old man's entire weight supported by his wife's one forearm. His skinny bare arse, the balls like these poor animal parts: shrunken, vulnerable in their slackened casing. Later, at home, his hoarse voice calling in the night. Her mother's distaste at his wasting body, the ghostly mind. A storm gathers force in Verla, and there is her mother's disgust about Andrew. Verla standing before her judges in the party president's office, sobbing, shaking. Her mother's sneering at them, *Good god, in France this would be nothing*, but really the disgust was for her, Verla, her daughter, once they were sitting in the car park in the dark. *What a cliché you are*. She said this to her daughter, then got on a plane and left.

Verla's father lies somewhere, afraid. Her horse too, afraid, trapped or sick somewhere. Death is coming to them all now—except Boncer, who should die, but he lives and they have killed this creature instead.

She feels the cold wind coming from the sky, and begins walking back down the hill.

Afterwards, Yolanda did not flinch as she cut the foot away.

THE SMELL of raw meat is in the air the next morning when Nancy is found dead in her bed. Lydia and Izzy report that Teddy sat on the filthy sheets gripping Nancy's jaw in one hand, weeping and fingering out white sludge and pill crumbs from her poor dead mouth.

Haunches and lumps of kangaroo hang in the shade of the veranda by the scullery, dripping onto the wooden boards.

• • •

The cockatoos wheeled and cried out in the dawn as the deep blue of the sky began to lighten.

Nancy was dead.

In her dogbox Yolanda lay in her rabbity nest and, for the first time in many long months, missed Robbie. She missed laying her cheek against the hard barrel of his chest, against his raspy sweaters. She missed his strong arms coming round her, fastening her to his body and swaying her in time with his own while they watched the football or stood beside his car in his mother's front yard.

Yolanda turned in her skin blankets and stared out at the fading stars.

Teddy had left Nancy there on her bed and stumbled away into the dry paddocks with his arms wrapped about his head, as if to protect himself from a beating. From the veranda the girls watched him go, saw the figure of him weaving up the slope, dark against the yellow land, and they heard the sound of an adult man's sobbing carrying to them for hours on drifts of air across the fields. Robbie had cried like that, unreachable, when Yolanda told him what had happened. And then he got up from her couch and walked away and did not speak a soft word to her again through all that followed.

She still missed him. She allowed herself to wonder, briefly, if he missed her. The old her, that was, the Yolanda of a lifetime ago. If Robbie saw her now he would not recognise her as his once-loved girl. He would curl his lip in revulsion and murmur to a mate, *Christ, check that out, would you hit it?*, and they would laugh into the open tops of their beer bottles as they turned away.

• • •

All day the girls collect kindling, gather the driest grass stalks and gum leaves they can find. They bundle up thick sticks and shreds of bark, all for the burning of Nancy. Verla walks the paddocks, snatching up tiny twigs and dragging old half-buried fence posts from the earth. Maitlynd emerges from under the house trailing long pieces of floorboard and plank behind her like a bridal train, and Leandra hauls some large hunks of rotten branch from her protected stove-wood pile. The heap of stuff grows higher.

At last, they bring poor Nancy. Izzy and Barbs carry her between them, wrapped in the dirty sheet from the sick-bay bed. They do not struggle to carry her weight, for Nancy stopped eating several days ago and her body is as light as a child's. Inside the sheet she is naked: they have taken away and burned already the boiler suit, and they washed her as best they could on the bed, scrubbing with a rag the odorous hollows of her armpits, between her thighs, behind her knees and ears. They wiped her stained face, cleaned away the crusts of vomit and smoothed her brow. They washed and combed back her hair.

Now all the girls gather round. They take corners and edges of the sheet and haul Nancy up and onto the pile of sticks and wood, lifting the rolled-sheet cocoon like a stretcher, pulling and tugging until she is laid out in the centre of the pile. She is unwrapped then, her little bruised body exposed to the sky, the pale soft skin over her frail frame, the patch of thick pubic hair startlingly black beneath those sharp hipbones. Her head tilts back, her scaly lips just parted. Already her face looks skeletal, the sallow skin taut over the cheek and brow bones. The dry blonde tails of her hair spread out from her skull, tangling in her springy bed of sticks and twigs.

The girls sit by the fire through the morning and all afternoon.

They have hated Nancy, wished her dead, laughed without mercy when they knew she suffered. But now she lies there in her girl's bare skin, they see she is only one of them, just skinny bone and sunken flesh, and for the first time they wonder if she has a mother too, somewhere in that little town she came from once, if somewhere a flatmate is still complaining about her unpaid rent, if the hot-bread shop owner ever asked where Nancy went.

As the day crawls on and the fire burns, the girls huddle closer together, arms about each other's shoulders. Tending the fire, keeping watch, holding vigil. Joy sings, clear and low, and Barbs and Izzy join in, their thin high off-key voices trying to harmonise in little hymns made of the joined-up songs of Rihanna and Gaga and Lana Del Rey. Maitlynd and Lydia turn their faces away and cry softly into each other's shoulders as the flames take hold, as Nancy's white skin slowly begins to darken and crackle, and burn.

They have to keep stoking the fire, adding branches and dried thistle stalks and lengths of timber fencing dragged from the collapsing sheep yard in the dusk. By the time the sky darkens with cloud and a few large raindrops pat down, the fire is burning deep and rich and will not be stopped. Verla and Yolanda sit together, cross-legged on the ground, waving smoke from their faces. After a time their hands find each other on the dusty grass. Verla watches the flames and knows finally what Yolanda knows. The realisation has been coming all along: her midnight horse was never real, was never going to save her.

Some hours after darkness falls, Hetty comes to stand and watch at the outer edge of the ring of girls, her eyes enormous. She stands apart, hands by her sides. For once she does not carry Ransom. Though Hetty has done nothing to Nancy they all know she is guilty, for she is Boncer's girl.

And more. Lydia and Joy nudge and whisper to each other, nodding at the growing curve of Hetty's belly protruding beneath the hem of Lydia's grubby T-shirt. Funny how clearly visible it is now, how the firelight finally confirms it, here in the quiet as Nancy burns. One body disintegrates in flame and another forms in water, cell by cell by duplicating cell, and Hetty stares into the fire, standing alone.

Neither Boncer nor Teddy comes out of the house, not even to watch from the veranda. Here, laying the dead to rest, like washing and feeding and birth, is women's work.

IT WAS not a bird call after all.

Yolanda looked up from where she squatted with the traps. Since the kangaroo she went out on her own again each morning. She did not want Verla's company, and Verla no longer followed her. The kangaroo's death had destroyed something between them, and Verla no longer spoke about her night horse. Yolanda was stealthy in the early dawn, the traps dangling from her belt, the comforting rhythm of chinking steel against her hip. She welcomed the dew now the weather was warming, lapping at her hem, soaking her thighs as she strode through the long grass.

Yolanda had felt something strange just before the bird's call—something had passed across her then vanished, like a smatter of the lightest summer rain over her face. Was it happiness? It could be, alone here with her work.

She came to the first trap now and kneeled to her daily prayer at the stiff furred body, knowing it as her own kind. She could merge, soon, with the ground itself, and there was so much longing in that knowledge, that sweetly speckled hallucination. Like those people who died in snow, the temptation to sink and sleep in the murderous ground must be resisted. Why? She did not know, except her instinct told her: *resist*. Resist.

That was when she heard the new bird call and looked up towards it from her place down in the shallow valley. And she saw it was no bird, but knew it for a long, lonely human cry. A figure was moving up the distant hill. A calico smudge tracing its way, a little grubby star trickling uphill, letting out that strange owl's cry.

Another Yolanda might have responded differently; the old Yolanda might have dropped the traps and shouted, called out, as she had with the balloon. But she knew that little smudge was Hetty, clambering and scrambling. The stolen clothes discarded, the old prisoner's tunic on her again. Yolanda knew the chaotic breaths and sobs that would be coming out of her as she climbed, the painful work of breathing and crying, the shimmering fear in her. She knew the direction Hetty was taking—up the ridge, up the bald stony track that Boncer had marched them that first day.

Later, Yolanda would go up there with the others, carrying a shovel.

She watched Hetty's slow crawl up the hill, growing smaller and smaller until she disappeared. Yolanda stood, observing her own stillness, watching herself not running back to the yard, not raising the alarm, not giving chase, not trying to save Hetty. The Yolanda who might once have done those things—who ran after the balloon, real or mad dream—that Yolanda might also at least have whispered, *Goodbye, Hetty*, but she did not whisper anything. She stood with her hands on her hips, watching until Hetty was gone. Then she breathed out a long, quiet exhalation and dropped back into her crouch, put her hands to the little body in the trap and released its crushed foreleg. She turned and stroked the creature before undoing her belt, threading the leather strap through the slit she'd cut into the rabbit's leg between muscle and bone, and rebuckled it around her waist.

She took the trap and teased the hair and fine shattered bone and the blood off the steel jaws with a certain tenderness, as if this perhaps might be Hetty, already returned to the earth and transformed, having offered up to Yolanda the rich warmth of her skin, the protein of her flesh, the useful pharmacology of her guts and mashed brain. She had given herself once before, why not now?

These things made Yolanda strong and let her know her time here was coming to an end. Sometimes when she thought about the end she grew a little empty. Then dragged herself heavily back, as she did now, to the one quiet, animal triumph: survival. Nancy was gone, the rabbits had died, Hetty would die, and each of these other deaths meant Yolanda would go on.

• • •

Verla sees Boncer's face when Yolanda returns from the traps and speaks. She stalks in and tosses the rabbit bodies onto the scullery bench, runs a hand down her dress. She peers down at her chest and picks a trail of gizzard away from her dress, then says, 'Hetty's gone to the fence.'

Boncer whirls around. 'Fuck off,' he says, with only mild irritation, but reaches for his spear gun. He yells at Izzy to go and fetch Hetty. She looks at Yolanda, and scurries out. They all know something is up: the air has gone tight. When Izzy returns she's bug-eyed. She makes sure to stand at a distance from Boncer's spear gun when she holds out Ransom to him by one rotting arm and says, 'Can't find her.'

Boncer is pale and swallowing strangely. He tucks the spear gun into his armpit and takes Ransom into his arms, staring at

Izzy. He holds the doll against his chest like a baby, as Hetty used to do.

• • •

Yolanda led the way, marching with the shovel carried across her chest. Boncer trudged behind her, Ransom clutched beneath one arm, the spear gun upright in the other. Then Verla and the rest of the girls, and Teddy at the end.

When they found her, her hands were still gripped around the wires of the fence, though her head lolled back now. She hung there, bowing and bending the wires. Verla looked past the strange stiff body of Hetty at the world beyond the fence.

Yolanda turned to the earth, ploughed the spade into it.

Boncer and Teddy had brought rubber gloves, taken from Nancy's sick bay. Teddy for once wore his rubber-soled work boots. The fence ticked and hummed. They each took up a wooden stick, and in an instant Hetty's body was levered off the fence, falling to the soft yellow grass with a thud. Teddy threw his stick down and stepped away, folding his arms. He would not go near another body after Nancy.

Boncer crouched by Hetty, the doll still in his arms. He stared tearfully at the destroyed body, the buckled skin. He would not touch her. The girls gathered round her, at first afraid to touch her little blackened hands like kangaroo paws, her face discoloured and distended, her hair singed.

Behind them, Yolanda lifted the spade and shunted its sharp blade into the hard ground, again and again.

Back at the house Leandra had found their old clothes stuffed into her oven: the red jacket, even the Chloé boots, all charred, wrecked, irretrievable. It was one more thing to hate Hetty for—but now they had her little body here, beneath their hands, they could not hate her. They went to work, worrying away at the body in silence, removing Hetty's clothes. The burnt patches of the tunic could be mended, her boots—Yolanda's old ones—were still better than most of theirs. Their hands worked over Hetty, industrious, unbuttoning and removing her dress, the socks, the underclothes they'd swapped with Hetty when she was given to Boncer. They searched her knotty dirty hair for hidden rubber bands or hairclips, ran their fingertips over her body for any remaining threads or hints of jewellery. They picked her over.

The hole was dug—not deep, but deep enough to cover her for now, until the dingoes came, or the hawks.

Yolanda was sweating. She straightened, grunting with the effort of the last shovelful. And then poor Hetty, heavier than the girls had expected, was awkwardly lifted, then dragged, curled and naked, to the edge of the hole. They tried not to graze her skin as they rolled her in. They looked away as Yolanda returned to the shovel and dropped the first rain of dirt down on Hetty in the ground.

Boncer stared down as Hetty was buried, the tears running down his face. He had attached Ransom sash-like across his chest as Hetty used to, and held the spear gun solemnly before him with two hands. It pointed straight up as if, were he a soldier with a rifle instead of clasping a spearfisher's stick, he might begin a twenty-one-gun salute.

Teddy hovered behind him, swaying a little, hands crossed at his groin in reverence. His eyes were bloodshot and his pupils enormous; he carried a little yellow tube of pills with him everywhere now, pulling it from his pocket now and then, flicking a pill or three into his mouth. As Boncer turned to walk back down the hill, Teddy put his arm about Boncer's shoulders—still carefully eyeing the spear gun—and offered him the pill bottle. Boncer unfurled his spare hand and mashed the pills into his mouth. They were brothers once more.

Yolanda turned to follow the procession of silent ragged girls, each carrying something of Hetty's, when she saw that Verla had trudged off alone along the fence line. She stood in the distance staring into the grass.

When Yolanda reached her, she was standing on the yellow earth, rocking on her feet, staring at the ground in silence. At first Yolanda could not discern what held her gaze, what kept her rooted there, wavering in that terrible way. She put out a hand to Verla's arm—and then she saw. At Verla's feet in the grass was a swag of rotting grey canvas. The submerged, decomposing ribcage of a horse lay half buried in the ground, still partly covered in a hide as pale and mottled as the face of the moon.

Verla turned to Yolanda and sobbed against her strong musty body, and Yolanda cradled her and rocked and cried with her, staring down at the pewter bone-cups of the hoofs, the sagging balloon of the belly, the long, noble jaw of the head decaying into the earth. It stared up at them from the round black hollow of its empty eye.

• • •

Afterwards, as the procession makes its way down the hill, leaving Hetty in the cold ground and the white horse decomposing in the grass, fresh silver lines come spangling into Verla's mind.

I do not ask who you are, that is not important to me.

It is as if cold mercury is seeping into her veins. She doesn't know these words, but she knows where they are from.

281

You can do nothing and be nothing but what I will infold you.

The understanding slowly comes. That Verla's self, that true naked self she had unwrapped and offered up, the self she had thought so particular, so vividly unlike any other, was not . . . seen. Andrew was not seeking her now, because he never did. In his every moment with her, his every act, it was his own self he saw and coldly worshipped. The mercury spreads through her, icy, unstoppable. She was an empty space to be occupied. When she was gone he would find another. Has already done so.

This knowledge comes in, clear and burning white: a constellation distinguishing itself from all the surrounding stars.

THIS NEW constellation still glitters at the centre of her when, that evening, Verla serves up the death cap to herself.

Her feet on the cool linoleum, she stands before the ancient stove top and shakes a pan in which the torn-up death cap rolls and sears. She was careful to pick it up with towelled hands. Now it is in the pan, hissing as its juices spread, it is benign. Surely this little thing cannot do what she wishes. *To cease upon the midnight with no pain*, except there will be pain, all right. She fears the pain. Oh, yes. She begins to cry a little again as she jiggles the pan. The others all have their plates, are eating already. They will all survive, Boncer too. This afternoon, after they buried Hetty, he pointed his spear gun at Izzy and ordered her into his room.

It is only a matter of time until Yolanda is taken, till they all are, but Verla has lost the will to survive, to outlast. She is so tired of all this striving, and it is only a small dull surprise that it is not Boncer's life that will end this way, but hers.

The butcher-boy puts off his killing-clothes.

She tips the mushrooms onto her plate. A glaze comes over her as she moves through the syrupy darkness of the hallway, into the ref. She takes her place at the table. Until this moment she does not know if she will say goodbye to Yolanda. But no, she will not. She wonders, dreamily, if Yolanda will come and cry at her bedside again, as her liver begins to fail. Will she hold Verla's head while she vomits blood, will she wrap her in rabbit and kangaroo skins, kiss her cold hands, try to smear the jaundice from her skin, her yellow eyes?

Across the table Yolanda slurps on rabbit juice, not looking anywhere but her plate. She is almost all animal now. She will not wrap Verla in her precious skins, will not hold her hand. It doesn't matter. Verla stares at the little brown pieces on her plate, the secret waiting for her. Something like peace is mixing in now with her fear, she can feel it creeping up through her body. H A R D I N G S, she reads, and it will soon be over. She takes up her fork and closes her eyes.

When she opens them she is looking at the bare table. Boncer has snatched her plate away. Her mouth opens to cry out but Boncer is muttering something hateful to her, the words muffled by his gobbling. He has speared half of it into his wet red mouth. She stares at him, and her cry has turned to a low groan, moving from her throat into her own belly.

And then Verla is shot back from death into living, forced up and up, bursting through its surface, gasping, into air: Boncer will die. At last, he will.

Will he, though?

She sits immobilised, watching his every movement, arranging her face, breathing in the violet air as the world outside this room grows dim. Her chest dissolves from the inside, the crust of a sandbank carved out by water. Boncer swallows, spears another slice into his mouth, and swallows again.

Outside in the evening a wattlebird wrenches pieces from the brush tree at the end of the veranda. Wrenching and ripping, rhythmic, just like her old familiar horse. Verla's limbs begin to flood. The relief—fear?—is an opened sluice in her, and with the flood comes a noise, a wheeze perhaps, or muted moan, and now Boncer stops chewing, suspicious. But he is already licking the taste from his lips, his derisive gaze sliding over Verla as he forks another mouthful in, fondling the doll with his other hand. None of them know what has happened except Verla, and she does not believe it. She has entered a lost white space, hears odd music and cicadas outside; the wrenching, ripping bird. Once she saw a coloured lizard's neck-frill flare stiff and shrink flat, flare and shrink. This world is spinning through time, like a fast-forwarded scene of evolution: black space, water shifting, sludge becoming amoebae becoming fish becoming all sorts, giraffes and man and moon landings and computers and the lizard frilling and fading, frilling and fading, all leading up to this moment in time and space because Boncer will die.

Maybe.

He does not look as if he will die. He looks completely normal. He has swallowed it, definitely. All of it. Nothing has changed. He runs his finger around the plate, licks up the rabbit gravy. Leans back in his chair and sniffs, pulls at his nose. Dandles Ransom on his knee. Sucking his teeth and turning to croon something into the doll's psoriasis-stained leather neck.

The lizard frill flares and disappears.

Verla picks up the dishes, picks up her heart still beating its strange knowing thud, and carries them into the scullery, moving softly on her new killer's feet. She stands in silence at the sink, staring at the plate, not knowing what she has done, or hasn't. Yolanda has followed her in, and watches her with the frying pan, obsessively rinsing and rinsing with boiling water. Verla knows Yolanda has noticed. *Both killers now*, she thinks. Perhaps Yolanda thinks it too, but it will be the working of her rabbit mind, not her girl mind, and she says nothing to Verla.

Verla handles the frying pan in wonder; such an instrument! This is all it takes. Perhaps this is all it takes, this small battered pan in her hand. She behaves as if nothing has happened. Because nothing has happened.

In her new ghostliness she goes to her own dogbox, shuts the door, shoves the pan to the deep recess beneath the bed. She climbs into the filthy cradle of it, lying beneath her mildewed blanket in disbelief and wondering horror.

She has not thought what they will do once Boncer is dead.

• • •

She dreams of Hetty and that small mouldering thing inside her, dreams that Hetty walks the paddocks bleeding, then squatting and bearing tiny rabbit babies in the grass. Yolanda and Verla sit with her while she rubs and grunts herself into the earth, panting. They sit and stroke her back while she labours. *Sorry, Hetty*, they say, *sorry*, but she doesn't hear them, intent only on the work of being female.

• • •

In the morning Verla wakes with her pulse skimming. She lets herself out of the dogbox early, walks out into the morning and picks mushrooms as if everything is the same. In the distance Yolanda's silvery movement is visible as she goes about her work.

Verla takes her mushroom catch—only two small ones—back to the kitchen where the other girls are dawdling. Boncer is not there. But nor is Izzy. He is doing things to her in his room, Verla thinks. She peers up the dark hallway but hears nothing.

The clatter of dishes around her begins, the hollow sound of empty cardboard boxes crushing. The storeroom is completely empty, but the girls go through the house whenever they get the chance, opening cupboards and peering into cardboard packing cases, now and then yelping with triumph when they find a stray rat-nibbled packet of mothy cereal or broken noodles.

Verla moves through the air that has become a thick gel, bubbled with possibility. Someone pushes past her, she does not say anything. Stands at the window and looks out across the paddocks. She cannot see Yolanda now.

She will not speak, it would break the spell. Is he sick? Dead?

Izzy comes into the kitchen, sniffing, rubbing her rib. Verla's breath seizes. She will not ask. Izzy is rummaging through drawers, looking about. Verla will not ask. The lizard frill flares, quietens. Izzy says nothing, only rattles until she finds a spoon, then shuffles to the pile of chipped dishes, as if nothing has happened. Nothing has happened.

Then it comes, the great tide of failure comes surging in, the thing she has never considered, not for one moment: it was not a death cap. They were not death caps. It was an ordinary mushroom she fed Boncer. She would not even have killed herself. She lets out a muffled groan. The girls glance at her, at each other. 'What's up?' says Lydia, but Verla cannot answer. Existence has never been less tolerable than at this moment. She leaps to her feet, snatching at things, will run from here, now. Get to the fence like poor Hetty, grasp hold of it, let the surge of it frazzle her brain and smoke her flesh. It must end, now.

But Izzy is blocking the doorway, fidgeting, her hand on the frame. When Verla looks at her out of her failure, devastated, Izzy says, 'He's vomiting.'

HOW LONG does it take?

Will Boncer come hunting them in his raging sickness? When Verla tells them what she has done, all the girls lock themselves in their cells from the inside and wait. He does not come.

Do they gather silently outside his room to watch the spectacle? To watch him crawling about, shitting green and vomiting? Do they press their faces to the window glass, as gleeful as a circus to see him suffer? Do they go through his drawers and cupboards while he moans and thrashes in pain, and do they hand his possessions around, take everything? Is this what they have become?

Yes they do. Yes they have. Yes, and yes, and yes.

Except Yolanda, who hears their cackling, takes up her traps and disappears out into the paddocks.

• • •

After the first day none of the girls can watch Boncer's suffering any longer. But Teddy has taken fright. He seizes back his spear gun and stands guard over Boncer's failing form, ordering the girls to bring boiled water, nurse him. Izzy takes pity first, cleaning his arse, washing him in the tepid tank water, emptying his vomit bowls away. For two long days he begins, it seems, to recover—and then sickens again. They take shifts then, Teddy sitting in the corner pointing, commanding this or that with the spear gun, while the girls come and go, cleaning up, smelling the scent of approaching death. At first Boncer cries for Ransom, but later he nudges her off the edge of the bed, and the rotting fabric of her finally gives way.

Verla bends to gather up the pieces of the doll, its lolling head intact but the rest mostly rag now, and scattered grass and dust. As she lifts it from the floor a little dark nub, like a dried prune, makes a tocking sound as it falls and meets the floorboards.

Outside this room, back at the ref, the girls divide up Boncer's belongings. They share out the shiny flotsam of his stuff—an iPad (dead, of course). A satellite phone with a mildewed leather cover: dead too. The wallet with pictures of his family. 'His mother looks so normal,' Leandra says sadly, passing this mystery around. Joy wears his jeans and his red surf T-shirt till Teddy bellows and, spear pointing, orders her into the sick bay to undress. Then he keeps her in there with him each night, threatening her with the spear if she strays too far.

The bag with Boncer's laptop and Xbox stuff is shared out in shock, solemnly pored over. 'I remember this old shit!' whispers Rhiannon, turning the games over and over in her hand as reverently as holy cards. Even right back at the start, when there was electricity, there was nothing to play these on. A little wash of new shock comes over the girls: even Boncer hadn't known what he was coming to.

There is no more morphine left, Nancy took it all. The rest of the pills they try on him in the first days, but nobody knows what they're for. Some seem to make him sicker.

Some of the girls leave their dogboxes and move into the house, opening rooms they have never been in, making up beds on the old red couches they saw on the first day and never again till now. But Yolanda no longer comes into the house at all. She eats with her hands, sitting on the veranda, leaving bowls licked and bones scattered for the rats.

• • •

It is Verla who volunteers for the night shift, listening to Boncer's ragged breathing, his delirious whimpers for his mother. On the last night, as she lies slumped in a chair, she hears his breathing alter. His face is grey against the pillow, his lips dry and opened, his cheeks sunken. He already looks like a corpse and a smell—soft, rotting, like fruit turning—has been rising from him, but still he breathes. Now his shallow exhalations take on a rough irregular clatter. For a moment the breathing stops, and the air is quieter than it has ever been—and then it begins again, the air dragging in and out of his body.

Verla stands and watches, sorrowful. It has been inevitable, she whispers to him. This was always going to happen. It is as unstoppable as the seasons that Boncer will die. He has brought it on himself, but Verla cannot help taking his pale hand in hers, and holding it. The skin is dry and cool. It slides, loose over his bones. She thinks of all the times she held her father's sad old hand, and for a fleeting moment she holds Boncer's to her lips.

As if in echo of Boncer's dying breath, a vast, low sound rises up from beyond the room, as if the building itself is dying too. Then a slit of shocking white appears beneath the door.

Verla lets go of Boncer's hand and goes to the door, opens it to see lights flaring on all through the house.

The power has come back on.

Boncer dies quietly, alone, while the girls run shrieking up and down the corridors.

AT FIRST they cannot not look up, scampering through the rooms beneath the glare of the fluorescent tubes, hands cupped over their brows. It is so bright!

It is a *sign*, Joy says when she comes into the ref, where the girls have gathered, blinking and staring. Little Joy, sweating and breathless, holding the spear gun—shortened without its shaft—in her small hand. She doesn't even know how she did it, except when the lights came on she knew it was a sign and before she understood what she was doing she had leaped from Teddy's bed and found that thing and ploughed it into him.

Joy rubs at her shoulder above the dangling weapon. 'This thing fricken *recoils*.' She shivers, triumphant, grinning in her ragged dress. The tube of light blares down and there is blood, all right. She stares around at them, grinning out of her smooth little face, waiting for applause. 'It was just, like, a *reflex*,' she says. Her chest heaves, in, out, with what she has done in the still night air. Then she drops the spear gun to the floor, and wipes her bloody hands on her skirt, and her little body begins to shake all over.

The power coming back on means one thing, and they all know it. Hardings is coming.

• • •

They stayed up all night, walking the corridors, laughing, crying. Chattering or silent, taking up space, enthralled.

At the end of that night and through the next two days a quiet fell over the place, like the night before Christmas. It was an awe, filled with longing and wonder, as their old lives came seeping, then trickling, then hurtling back—the jobs, the streets, the houses where they lived. The boyfriends.

Would their families recognise them? Where would they live now? The outside world: *imagine*. Did it still exist? Would it receive them? Who would be waiting?

They had no idea how long they had been here.

None of this they spoke aloud, but as they trailed through the house freely now—lost, soon to be rescued—gradually they found themselves returning to their rituals: Leandra at the stove, Maitlynd clucking to her frog, Barbs with her stockpot.

Rhiannon crossing the paddocks to clamber once more into her skeleton ute.

Yolanda had never stopped roaming the paddocks, and barely came near the house.

Only Verla stopped her mushroom hunt. She sat on the veranda in the weak sunlight, staring into the air.

Joy and Lydia and Izzy cleaned up the messes of Boncer and Teddy and left them on their beds, combed their hair, folded their hands like saints. Had to leave the spear shaft in Teddy, packing rags around it so it grew out of his chest like a warrior flower. Izzy wanted to use the spear gun on Boncer's head too but they talked her down: *You'll never get over doing that, Iz. Have it in your brain forever, you don't want that.*

The folder of Incident Reports they gathered and read in silence around the ref table. How Boncer had reduced Hetty, that was unforgivable. They had believed even he had loved her, in his strange dreadful way. She was carrying his baby. And now here was his cramped schoolboy lettering, making her as small as three words. *Client suicide: electrocution.* Lydia was solemn, too, after her search of all the rooms and every drawer and cupboard. All their real clothes burned by Hetty, it was true. Nothing of their old lives remained.

How were they to prepare for freedom?

These last nights were crazed with celebration. Even Yolanda came inside to eat, and Izzy flung the bowls of stew to the table, singing that soon they would never have to eat mushroom-fucking-rabbit-fucking stew ever again! They cheered, whooping. Some began to chant: *Hardings is coming! Hardings is coming!* They made a little song, and Joy and Rhiannon danced ring-a-rosie around the table.

Only Yolanda did not smile, but nibbled on pink rabbit flesh and grunted, as if she always had been this way.

And now the girls turned to look at Yolanda, beheld her in her stinking bloody skins, eating with her blackened hands, ripping meat from bone. Who was going to want that, back in the world? Glances were exchanged, smirks covered with hands. Imagine that filth in an apartment, an office. Imagine Yolanda *shopping*. They began giggling.

Yolanda did not appear to notice. She took up the Incident Report pad and started scrawling on it with her mudstained paws.

THE NEXT afternoon, as they know they will, they hear it coming. A cry goes up, the girls go running to the veranda to stand and watch the tiny vision of the yellow coach winding down from the ridge, disappearing into the scrub, appearing again in flashes through the black trees. Its lumbering progress over the grass, around the dam, crushing all things.

The line of girls. Tangle-haired, dirty, skinny. Their body hair grown, their breasts slumped and low, hips wide or narrow, wild creatures such as they have never been in the ordinary world.

The yellow coach appears and disappears, angular through the tussocks, along the gravel road built by the girls. Its faint sound growing.

Yolanda is not in the line. Verla has been looking for her since dawn, out in the paddocks, all through the outbuildings and storerooms, the house and the dogboxes. The bus drones louder, and Verla runs through the house once more, then stumbles down to the dogboxes, calling and calling for Yolanda.

When she enters Yolanda's box for the third time, she finds it bare. All the skins gone. No piles of little bones or shreds of fur.

She has not even said goodbye.

Verla looks around for a scrap, something to take, but the room is empty of everything that was Yolanda. From the road the bus's rumbling comes. Verla's heartbeat is quickening. It is time to go. She takes a last look around the empty box, turns out of the door, and steps straight into Yolanda.

Yolanda stands, breathing steadily, belted and laden with skin blankets, traps, a dangling knife. She nods at Verla and jerks her head towards the fields, holding out her dirty mittened hand. Verla stares. The bus is coming.

At home her father waits in his chair, his ghost hand waving. At home there are the soft jetty boards, the glinting water.

'Quick,' whispers Yolanda. They can both hear the bus, coming over the rutted gravel road.

Verla finds Yolanda's fingers inside the furred gauntlet and takes her hand. She looks into the small dark animal eyes and says, 'I want to go home.'

They stand in the dark corridor of the dogboxes. Verla smells Yolanda's animal breath, feels the quick fine skeleton beneath her skin. She feels Yolanda's speedy heart drumming in the burrow of her chest. Yolanda gathers Verla to herself one last time, then lets her go. She pulls the bulky cape of her skins about her and pads to the end of the corridor, out of the doorway and disappears into the glaring light. Verla sprints from the boxes, scrambles back up to the veranda. She turns to see the low silver flash of Yolanda's skins only just visible, swift through the grass.

She is already far in the distance when the coach finally heaves up the slope towards the buildings, dust rising in its wake. It is vast and modern, lurid unnatural yellow, brutally mechanical before them. HARDINGS INTERNATIONAL in small black lettering, clean and sharp along its side, as it nears.

The coach jerks to a stop, the long hiss of its hydraulics sighing in the silence. The dust smoking up and hanging in the air. After a moment, the door slowly opens.

A man—shaven, fatherly, in a clean blue uniform—steps down, calling out to them. 'Hello, ladies, how are you this afternoon?' He is so unmarked, so clean, has come from a land so far away.

Then he sees them, their mess and damage. He says softly, looking along the line of them, 'What have we got here? Dear, oh dear.' The girls shift, suddenly afraid, under his stare.

The man takes a step towards them. He says, 'You poor, poor girls.'

They stiffen, huddle closer together, stealing glances. *Poor girls*. The man steps back onto the bus, disappears for a moment, and emerges with a cardboard box. They strain to listen, but it is true, he has not said you sluts dogs fat slags bitches slurry. Said *poor girls*.

The girls can hear each other breathing. They hold hands, afraid. The man has put the box on the ground and he now begins to lift out a crisp parchment carry bag, then another and another, looping them over his wrist as he counts. The thick paper of the bags is powder-coated creamy white, embossed. You want to run your fingers over the pure untouched surface, along those sharp clean edges. You want to hold them, to feel the swing and tilt, because of the weight, the shadow of deep green tissue, inside.

The girls look about them, pressing together, trying to read the future in one another's stricken faces. They stand motionless, too afraid to step down from the veranda, from this rotting wooden island, their mouldering home. They can smell the man now as he bends into the box, rummaging. There is the rustle of tissue paper. His sweet chemical odour rises up at them, like liquorice, like cinnamon, like a memory of long, long ago when they once were clean, when they knew other clean people. How naked he looks to them. How newborn.

He steps towards them now, a clutch of the bags in each hand, twirling on their satiny black rope handles. The bags slither expensively against one another.

Even from here Verla sees how clinically pure the man's hands are, his nails clipped and pink. She curls her own into fists.

'I'm Perry, by the way,' he calls out across the dangerous ocean of mottled grass, and smiles. He stands in the sun. The bags slide against each other, alive, slippery, as glossy as racehorses. The girls cannot stop staring. At what? What is in those bags? A promise, a stirring of something: tenderness, ease, something from the history of love, far beyond this place.

It is Lydia who whispers, in disbelief, 'They look like Phaedra.'

Can't be.

Barbs knows. '*Real* Phaedra costs, like . . .' and can only shake her head, so no, it is not possible. But something is simmering, they all remember what Maitlynd told them one night, calling out from her bed. How her ex-boss once gave her a tiny Phaedra sample, and how *unbelievable*, even in that tiny amount, how like a *whole new skin,* she swore it. The girls look down, quickly, at their bitten, blackened hands.

The man is waiting with his patient smile, but he begins to look uneasy. He turns towards the bus, the bags swivel. The girls feel their bodies longing, surging towards him, though they don't yet move. Rhiannon murmurs, 'Maybe it's, like, a reward.' And now something dawns on Lydia, who used to work in charity events: 'Phaedra's maybe a Hardings partner.' They look at her. 'A *sponsor.*'

They cannot yet know, but what they see for certain is the unmistakeable embossed swirling P, some other smaller letters. And look, there again, the wisp of rich, deep turquoise tissue paper. Paper? More like silk, like an infinity pool. They each turn inwards, to their memories, their yearning, their long-ago breathtaken senses. Verla held the rich starched linen of that Paris hotel bed-sheet between her fingers. She put pastries of so many buttered layers in her mouth. And she stood in the street before the Louboutin window, that vertical slipper with its red needle heel poised in the glass dome like a jewel, a test tube, a syringe. Like a pharmaceutical thing to enhance you, heal you, cure you.

In the long-distant past, Teddy's and Boncer's cold hands were folded across their chests. They are old ghosts from dreams now, like Verla's dusty white horse, but here is the actual future, in a clean sharp uniform and a shining yellow bus, and in his hands these creamy parchment vessels bevelling sunlight. Verla just wants to *touch*, to run her finger along the perfect, knife-sharp pleat of that paper edge.

They cannot take their eyes from the bags.

Somewhere far behind them poor insane Yolanda is playing dirty animals. Still captive, twitching in the bush, shrugging into the leaves, digging, burrowing. Mad as shit.

It is Barbs who cannot, finally, wait any longer. It's big-boned Barbs who says to the man in a small, polite voice, 'Can I've a look?'

'Of *course*, love!' sings Perry, beaming, standing at the door of the bus now. Barbs (*of course, love!*) steps across the grass in her rotten leather boots, and gingerly takes a bag from his hands. They lean, nobody breathes, watching Barbs reach in, peering, and she cries, 'Oh!' and pulls out a heavy black glossy box, and she shrieks, 'It *is* Phaedra!' and they see its velvet innards, the cut-glass lid. Barbs presses it to herself, looks up at the girls, her face alight. And then it's all thundering off the boards, and they are squatting on the ground ripping open the little packages, not only Phaedra but, incredibly, from MarthaJones and Nyfödd and

NaturescienceSeries II, the man smiling benignly down while they cry out and unscrew bottles and squish creams into their hands and press sticky gloss to their flaking lips with their dirty fingers. Verla looks up for Perry, who is no longer on the grass with them but slipping into the house. 'Wait,' she hisses to the girls, but they are all squealing because Lydia's holding up a silver razor and hitching up her dress, looking down at her soft-furred legs and sobbing with grief and relief. They all dive into their bags for the shining thing and come up with it, a beautiful bullet, a scalpel in their hands. Verla's heart begins to beat too fast.

She stands and looks across the plains for Yolanda. She shades her eyes and traces with her gaze the plains, the curving hillside, the grassy paddocks, but Yolanda is nowhere to be seen, not with a human eye. And now Perry is back beside her on the grass with his perfumed, shaven male smell. 'Let's get you out of here,' he says and there is regret and pity in his voice. Like he knows what's been done to them here, and it must never take place again. Has he found Boncer and Teddy? He only beams again and does not even need to speak, for the girls have begun filing onto the bus, chattering and weeping, first looking behind them to the grass to make sure they have left nothing, lost none of their treasures. Their hands are filled with turquoise Phaedra tissue and gleaming white tubes and heavy glass vials, and they suck into their lungs the glorious, forgotten smell of flowers and herbs and money.

Verla puts her foot on the step, her unexplored bag dangling heavy and rich and scented from her wrist. From inside the bus Leandra is heard to scream, '*Chocolate!*' through her stuffed mouth. Verla hesitates an instant, but, 'Up you go, sweetie,' and Perry's hand is at her back propelling her, with too much strength, too expertly, too fast up the steps and now she is on board, inside the cool fresh tunnel of the bus, with all the others. And the door has closed behind them with a soft whumping breath, sealing them all in. Perry swings into the driver's seat and the engine roars into life. Each girl has dropped into a double seat—*how soft is it!*—and sits squawking in delight from her little nest of tubes and packets.

The bus begins to rock and surge off down the road the girls have built—*on our knees, with our hands*—away from the compound, and a seeping, a deathly bleeding of something rotten, starts up in Verla. She doesn't open her mouth, nor her bag. It sits, pure white, heavy across her knees. She stares through the tinted window, out across the paddocks, scanning the scrub. The sun is lowering in the sky. She cannot see her.

You poor girls.

The bus is filled with noise, the girls calling one to another like birds. Izzy has found a hairbrush at the bottom of her bag, and screeches, brandishing it, sending them all diving, and now they rake at each other's bird's-nest hair, and Leandra is scouring her face with citrus blossom cleansing wipes and gasping, *Jesus, fuck, look* at the dirt coming off. They hoot at their reflections in the window glass, *oh my god oh my god.*

The road becomes a lumpy track where they had run out of concrete and gravel and the bus slows, heaving and rocking from side to side as it lumbers up, up the stony hillside, up towards the ridge. And then it looms: the fence. Huge, black.

The girls are suddenly silent, open-mouthed as they press their foreheads to the tinted windows, each girl holding her breath to see if this is really happening. The bus slows, stops, juddering, while—nobody breathes—a massive wired panel of the fence slides, rumbling and rattling, open.

In this slow-motion moment only Verla moves, darting from one side of the bus to the other. There is only grey, scrappy scrub. The bus moves through the open gate. Verla hooks her hands around her face at the window, praying *please please*, and then she sees: a little furred figure sprinting low alongside the great wall of bus. And the little figure is through the fence and veers away, spinning low and fast as a rabbit off into the scrub.

Goodbye, Yolanda, Verla whispers to the glass. *Goodbye.*

The creamy bag with its silken ropes rests against the upholstery of the seat next to her. The air is fragrant, a little sickly now.

Verla reaches inside her tunic as the bus heaves off again, unpins a little grubby cloth and puts it in her lap. The seeping in her has not stopped with the closure of the gate behind them, and Verla knows now what to do.

Inside this pocket on her lap is the remaining death cap mushroom.

The sun is setting. The bus comes to a junction, and the girls are perched up on their seats now, all except Verla, staring in wonder at the long pale gravel road in both directions. Not yet a highway, but an actual *road*. The girls cheer and cheer, then burrow back into their treasures, not caring, not seeing that the bus turns west, not east. Not away from but into the setting sun. Verla sees Perry flick a look in the mirror at them, his cargo, then back to the dusty road.

The house with its dead bodies, the broken buildings, the dogboxes are far behind them now. Verla sees a swatch of birds glitter and turn in the sky. *You poor girls.* This Perry did not mean what had happened to them back there. He meant what was to come.

She unwraps the little cloth bag, breaks off a piece of mushroom and holds it with the cloth, in her fingers.

She needs to know what she is. She is a daughter, and she whispers sorry to her father as she sees herself doing it, putting this piece of mushroom in her mouth, chewing, mashing it up, resting her head against the vibrating window, swallowing. She closes her eyes and forgives her mother, says goodbye to her father. Says to Andrew, *Look for me under your boot soles*, and feels with no pain the plain small fact that he did not love her and never had.

The girls chitter in the seats behind her. Verla holds the little fatal mushroom piece in her hand and before she puts it to her tongue she calls through the scrub in her mind to Yolanda, her protector, fellow creature: *I love you.* I am your sister, and you are mine. And at last Verla knows herself loved. She presses the mushroom between her fingers, through the cloth.

But then Yolanda speaks back. Her voice comes from a fine grey blur spinning through the grass, across the plains, right into the centre of Verla, and it is not old dead Walt Whitman's voice she hears but the fresh, living rhythm of a beating heart, of surging blood and paws thrumming over the earth. Verla feels this pulse, urgently, in her body. The bus changes gear again, Perry rests back in his seat, settling in for a long drive ahead. And two words force their way through everything in Verla, pushing through all these months, through failure and fear and degradation, fighting through this last defeat. They thrust up through Verla's centre, bursting into flower in her mouth. Two words: *I refuse.*

She is on her feet, moving down to the front of the bus, swinging into Perry's face, startling him. 'Stop driving.'

She feels the air change behind her. The girls' squawking has quietened. The bus hums on, and Perry has to look up from the road. The sun is in his eyes, he squints beneath the visor. He says, 'There's a toilet at the back, love.'

Verla, louder: 'Stop. Let me off.'

Irritation crosses Perry's face before he turns a cold smile on her, his powerful hands gripping the huge black steering wheel. 'Just sit down, all right, love? It's against health and safety.'

But girls have begun moving down the aisle. He hears them, though he stares at the road, his face steely. 'Everyone *sit* down, please,' barks Perry.

Joy's voice rings out, pure above the motor's noise. 'Let her off.' The girls shift and bristle around her, around Verla. Perry glances into the mirror then back at the road, quietly angry now. But he has seen them in that glance, the girls standing there, looming, lit brilliant by the lowering sun. There are eight of them. Framed in his vision they stand: mud-streaked, teased-haired, some with horrible orange lipstick now, some with garish beads and ribbons. They have been made strong by labour and brutality. They are ablaze.

'*Get* back into your seats!' he yells, and he starts fumbling beneath the dash, but he's afraid, they can feel it, they know he has seen Boncer and Teddy back at the house.

Verla feels the wall of girls, the strength of their hard warm bodies at her back, standing with her. Suddenly Leandra darts in, yells, 'Hold on!' and yanks the steering wheel, making the whole bus tilt, swerve savagely on the dirt road.

'Jesus *fuck*!' bellows Perry.

• • •

When she has picked herself off the gravel—*die then, mental bitch*—Verla stands alone on the road, tasting the powder of dust in her mouth, the dry, dry air settling over her skin.

The water bottles the girls threw to her lie dented in the dirt. Her shoulder hurts like hell; her knees and forearms are bleeding, but not badly. The bus is gone. She looks back down the road, in the direction they came from.

She can have no possible idea where Yolanda is; she is already far away, fully animal, released. Thinking of Yolanda now, so vigorously alive in her rabbit self, Verla remembers that other self of her own, called up once in her fever dreams. That little brown trout, hovering motionless in the water, waiting.

She turns away from the setting sun and wipes her sleeve across her sweaty face. It will be dark soon, and will grow cold. It will be hard. She might die. She bends to gather the water bottles, shuffling in a circle in the pink dust. When she has picked them all up she begins trudging down the gravel road.

• • •

The little brown trout twitches, and is gone. Only the clear water moves in its wake.

ACKNOWLEDGEMENTS

THANKS TO those who helped me write this book, often without knowing it: Rebecca Hazel, Alison and Mary Manning, Ruby and Lily Johnson, Jane Doepel, Kerry and Deborah Bennett, the Bundanon Trust, my PhD supervisors at the University of New South Wales Anne Brewster and Dorottya Fabian, Joan London, Eileen Naseby, Lucinda Holdforth, Vicki Hastrich, Tegan Bennett Daylight, Ailsa Piper, Caroline Baum, Hannie Rayson, Stephanie Bishop, David Whish-Wilson and Curtin University. I thank all the writers who generously took part in *The Writer's Room Interviews*; each conversation has influenced my work in profound ways. Thank you to Jenny Darling, Jane Palfreyman,

Ali Lavau, Siobhán Cantrill, Clara Finlay, Lisa White, Stella Chambers, Andy Palmer and all at Allen & Unwin for their expert care. Always and most of all, thanks to Sean McElvogue.